T0392286

speed demon

speed demon

ERIN LYNN

BERKLEY JAM, NEW YORK

THE BERKLEY PUBLISHING GROUP
Published by the Penguin Group
Penguin Group (USA) Inc.
375 Hudson Street, New York, New York 10014, USA
Penguin Group (Canada), 90 Eglinton Avenue East, Suite 700, Toronto, Ontario M4P 2Y3, Canada
(a division of Pearson Penguin Canada Inc.)
Penguin Books Ltd., 80 Strand, London WC2R 0RL, England
Penguin Group Ireland, 25 St. Stephen's Green, Dublin 2, Ireland (a division of Penguin Books Ltd.)
Penguin Group (Australia), 250 Camberwell Road, Camberwell, Victoria 3124, Australia
(a division of Pearson Australia Group Pty. Ltd.)
Penguin Books India Pvt. Ltd., 11 Community Centre, Panchsheel Park, New Delhi—110 017, India
Penguin Group (NZ), 67 Apollo Drive, Rosedale, North Shore 0632, New Zealand
(a division of Pearson New Zealand Ltd.)
Penguin Books (South Africa) (Pty.) Ltd., 24 Sturdee Avenue, Rosebank, Johannesburg 2196,
South Africa

Penguin Books Ltd., Registered Offices: 80 Strand, London WC2R 0RL, England

This book is an original publication of The Berkley Publishing Group.

PRINTING HISTORY
Berkley JAM trade paperback edition / November 2008

Library of Congress Cataloging-in-Publication Data

Lynn, Erin.
    Speed demon / Erin Lynn.—Berkley JAM trade paperback ed.
        p. cm.
    Summary: Grounded for having used her mother's minivan to close to demon portal, sixteen-year-old Kenzie is grounded and must spend even more time with demon Levi, who informs her that when she closed one portal she opened another and it is up to her to save the day—again.
    ISBN 978-0-425-22366-6
    1. Demonology—Fiction. 2. Cats—Fiction. 3. High schools—Fiction. 4. Schools—Fiction.
5. Family life—Ohio—Fiction. 6. Ohio—Fiction. I. Title.
    PZ7.L993Spe   2008
    [Fic]—dc22

                                                                                                2008027328

147204767

Chapter One

You'd think I was the first sixteen-year-old ever to drive a minivan through the kitchen the way my parents were acting.

Seriously. It's had to have happened before. Somewhere. Maybe. For reasons clearly not as good as mine.

But instead of credit—hello, I did save my family from being overrun by demons—I got yanked out of sleep. At seven a.m. on a Saturday. Does that sound even remotely fair to you?

Me neither.

But there was no denying that there was the most obnoxiously loud banging sounds coming from downstairs, jack-hammering straight into my head and making it absolutely impossible to sleep.

Yep. Reconstruction had started on the kitchen wall that

imploded when I hit it with my mom's van and closed the demon portal.

On a Saturday. At seven a.m.

Putting a pillow over my head didn't help one flipping bit, and I knew that at eight my mother was going to wake me up to help her chaperone my little sister's Daisy Girl Scout meeting (part of my punishment for the minivan through the wall), so it seemed futile to force sleep, anyway. The minute I got back into REM, she'd be ripping the blanket off my head.

Trying to talk and yawn at the same time as I shuffled down the stairs twenty minutes later, I pulled the hood of my sweatshirt over my dark hair, the dyed pink tips sticking out and poking me in the mouth. "Why is this Girl Scout meeting so early?" I asked my mother, who was trying to fill the coffeepot from the bathroom sink. "Eight a.m. on a Saturday should be illegal."

There were several strange and random men wandering around our kitchen, and the source of the banging became apparent when I saw one of them was knocking pieces of drywall out of the damaged wall. That seemed a little counterproductive. They were supposed to be fixing it, not destroying it even more. I shifted to the other side of the island, aware that I was still in pajama pants and that the one construction dude looked like he was on the short side of twenty. Big and brawny, he was staring at me.

I knew that look. It was the prologue to flirting and I so didn't want to go there. He had shoulders wider than my bedroom door and hair that looked like it had suffered an accidental encounter

SPEED DEMON

with his electric saw. Not my type. Not even in the same genus, let alone species, as my preferred dating category.

The water to the kitchen had been shut off for the momentous start of Kitchen Wall Repair (this event was to repeat every day for the next three weeks), and it was making my mother more than a little edgy not to have easy access to her morning caffeine. There were vicious and impatient clanking sounds as she tried to maneuver the pot under the bathroom faucet to fill it.

"Kenzie, I really don't want to hear it," she snapped at me.

What? It was a simple question. No need to bite my head off. "You know you could just fill a glass then use that to fill the coffeemaker," I pointed out.

She glared at me from the open bathroom door, my helpful hint obviously not appreciated. "Go make sure your sister is awake."

I wanted to say something sarcastic, but didn't dare. I was currently not my mother's favorite person (see six-page itemized construction bill for Kitchen Wall Repair lying on my father's desk), and I figured that I was going to have to just ride out the horror of being grounded in agonizing silence.

"And throw in a load of laundry when you come down!" she called after me as I stomped up the stairs to arouse my five-year-old sister from her beauty sleep so I could stand around and watch her and a pack of squealing friends twist yarn around Popsicle sticks. And my mother needed my help for that, why? Not exactly my idea of a happening time for a Saturday morning. Saturday is for sleeping. For shopping. For calling my boyfriend,

Adam, and spending lots of time listening to him describe all the ways he adores me.

That sounded like a much better use of my time, but the problem was, given that parents were parents, I couldn't exactly announce that I saved them from demon servitude, so the end result was servitude for me. Also known as Being Grounded.

The anatomy of a Grounding for the offense of driving car through kitchen wall was as follows:

- No driver's license until I was eighteen (whimper).

- No allowance for a year, to make up for the five-hundred-dollar deductible on crushed front end of minivan. (Dad said there was no way to make up for the cost of the kitchen and that instead of a two-hundred-guest wedding hosted by him in ten years, I would now have to hold my reception in our kitchen as it had cost the same as a wedding.)

- No going out with Adam unsupervised. (Like I was going to agree to supervision? Please.) Though he was allowed to come over in two-hour blocks.

- No going out in any capacity for four weeks. (Think of all the movies and parties that would sail by without me. Tragic.)

- Saturday servitude for three months. (Do anything my mother or father demanded which so far had involved lots of laundry, dishes, and now assisting Daisy Troop 1347.)

Like I knew anything about corralling a group of five-year-olds. But I could play along. Technically, if I wanted to be rational about it, it was sort of almost a fair grounding. I guess I wouldn't be thrilled if my kid took out the kitchen wall either, though I'm not sure that I would be so utterly cruel as to deny her a driver's license for eighteen months. The loss of a future wedding reception didn't really bother me—I could slap on a pair of jeans with a white dress and have a rockin' wedding in the park if I ever decided I was going to actually take that step. And I could wiggle around the no-dating-Adam thing if they dragged that out for too long. Cleaning the house, okay, fine, whatever.

But the driver's license? That hurt. What, like they'd never had a fender bender? And of course I was stuck accepting all consequences, sucky as they may be, because I couldn't exactly explain to my mother that not only had I driven the minivan through the kitchen, I had in fact *meant* to do it. My parents would be calling up the Horizons Psychological Center and admitting me if I said that I had driven the car into the wall to close a demon portal that had opened in my shower when I dropped my acne meds down the drain.

Parents tend to be a little reactionary about things like premarital sex, recreational drugs, and demonic activity. It wouldn't matter that I wasn't doing the first two, they would hone in on my paranormal problem and pack me off to psych prison.

No thanks on that. I had plans for the rest of the fall and they didn't include a fashion-forward snap-up hospital gown and Dixie cups filled with a rainbow of pills.

So the demon thing was a secret, and it would have been really easy to pretend that it had never happened, despite the reconstruction on the kitchen wall, if the source of all my original problems wasn't living in my house and currently strolling out of the room he shared with my brother, Brandon.

"Morning, K," Levi said, looking wide-awake and cheerful.

Demons shouldn't be chipper. It should be a rule. Or maybe just my rule. Rule Number 1: Levi must never be perky in my presence. I needed to work on enforcing that.

"Hey." Morning never made me feel wide-awake and pleasant on a good day, and at the moment I was feeling doubly bitter.

"What has you so bent?" he asked.

"Nothing." There was no point in explaining it to Levi, because he didn't have to live under the same restrictions I did. He had no parents, an obscenely easy class load at school, a driver's license, and the demonic ability to coax people to do what he wanted. What did he know about being Kenzie Sutcliffe? Nothing. Exactly. That would be correct.

Do I sound a little whiny? I try not to be, but you know, sometimes you just can't help feeling seriously sorry for yourself, like when you try on bathing suits or when you get dumped or when your best friend is suddenly hot and heavy with some random dude and you're left in her dating dust. This was one of those days. I was just feeling like I'd gotten a bit of a raw deal.

"Okay, whatever," he said, pretending to look hurt. "No reason to confide in me, your friend, who loves you like a sister."

My raw deal was named Levi Athan.

Annoying from day one, he had appeared in my shower (I wasn't in it at the time, *thank God*) and proceeded to become the new It guy at school, despite the fact that he was in fact a demon (but not a totally evil one) escaped from demon prison. Not that anyone knew any of that but me, which somehow made it all worse. Now I was stuck with him living in my house and having every girl crushing on him while I took the fall for closing the demon portal.

I did close the demon portal, as noted earlier, but did I mention I did it all by myself? With no help from Levi, who was the otherworldly entity here? Yep. All by my little bitty self. You'd think that would earn some respect from him, but so far it hadn't surfaced.

I gave him an eye roll and moved past to drag Zoe's little carcass out of bed. Fortunately, that proved easy enough since she was already awake and searching through her closet in her pink satin nightgown.

"I can't find my denim miniskirt," she said as a greeting, desperately digging through a pile of clothes on the floor. "Help me look, Kenzie."

"You're hanging around our house with a bunch of other girls," I said, halfheartedly glancing around the room. "Just wear something else."

Zoe shot me a look of utter disbelief. "But it goes with my black boots and striped tights, which I'll *die* if I don't get to wear."

My sister, the five-year-old fashionista. She was my mother's great hope for future homecoming queen.

"Right, of course. We can't have you croaking. That would really ruin my Saturday." I picked through a pile of clothes on her zebra-striped chaise and was amazed at the vast quantity of studded, appliquéd, and sequined clothes Zoe had. She had enough glitter to hit the stage in Vegas. I pulled my black hoodie a little tighter around me for comfort. So much pink and gold glaring up at me was totally traumatizing.

A very tiny and short skirt with scrolling hearts on the pockets appeared and I tossed it to Zoe. She'd better be wearing tights with that thing or she'd be pulling a Britney. "Thick tights, Zoe. That is a short skirt."

"It's a skort," she informed me disdainfully, lifting the flap on the skirt to reveal the little shorts underneath.

Feeling much better and like maybe my sister's future didn't include dancing in a bikini for money, I went back downstairs only to hear Levi talking to my mother.

"If you need extra help with the girls, Mrs. S, I can hang around."

Who volunteers to make crafts with a Girl Scout troop at the crack of dawn on a Saturday?

"Oh, that's so sweet of you, Levi. I'd love some extra help."

A suck-up, that's who.

"I think it's just wonderful that you don't complain, Levi. You just dive in whenever help is needed. I appreciate that."

Was that a dig at me? Hey, I was grounded. I wasn't supposed to be happy about that. That was just too much to expect from any teenager who wasn't taking antidepressants.

"They'll be here in fifteen minutes," she added, and breezed out of the kitchen with a smile for Levi, who she thought was just such a nice boy.

Teenage boy . . . demon from hell. I guess it's not really that different, is it? But it was irritating that I seemed to be the only one who saw through Levi's over-the-top Nice Guy routine. He wasn't all sweetness and light, I'm telling you.

As was evidenced by the smirk he was giving me. "I'm appreciated," he told me.

"Glad someone feels that way," I commented.

"That's your problem," he said. "You should appreciate me, but you don't."

"I'd appreciate you more if you lived in someone else's house."

I thought he would sling another barb my way, but instead he actually came up to me and wrapped his long arms around me and gave me a hug. "Poor Kenzie. It sucks being grounded, I know. I'm sorry."

Awwww. How sweet was that? Okay, true confession here. I actually sort of liked Levi. He made me laugh, and he really was actually a nice guy (demon) for the most part when he wasn't being obnoxious (aka Every Guy I've Ever Met). "Thanks, Levi."

I rested my head on his chest and put my arms loosely around his middle, staring at his chin with its wispy stubble. Levi wasn't as muscular as Adam. (Did I mention Adam is my boyfriend? If I did, so what, it bears repeating. Frequently.) But it was nice to lean on Levi and think of him as a friend. When we weren't giving each other a hard time, we really did get along.

"Man, you have morning breath," he murmured. "You'd better run up and brush before you knock anyone out."

Nice. So much for being tight with him. And for the record, I already had brushed and flossed. I pulled back and spoke extra loud, with lots of forced air right into his face. "*Sorry.*"

I saw the young construction hulk glance over at us, and I moved a little closer to Levi. There was something about that guy that freaked me out. He was just so . . . big.

Levi grinned. "I'm kidding, you know."

"I know. It's a totally male behavior to use insulting humor when he's uncomfortable with his own display of emotions." Wow. I had actually learned something in psychology that could be applied to real life. When does that ever happen with forced knowledge? I tried to pull away to escape to my room but he held me tighter.

"Exactly. You may not appreciate me, but you understand me."

Um . . . why was Levi looking at me like that? Sort of intense and amused and intrigued, and when exactly had his leg started touching mine? Were we really that close to each other?

"I do understand how your demonic mind works." Sort of. I opened my mouth to blow another steady stream of alleged morning breath right into his face to make him laugh or grimace— either would be rewarding—when he leaned over.

And kissed me.

What the . . . ?

You know what it's like when you totally don't see something coming and you're caught off guard, so you just stand there blinking with your mouth wide open?

That's what I did. He was kissing me, and I was gaping and blinking for a solid ten seconds.

Then an incredibly weird thing happened that while I can explain biologically, I can't explain intellectually, because I can't ever imagine that if my brain had actually been functioning independently of my body, what happened next would have gone down. But guys use hormones as an excuse for like ninety-five percent of their behavior so I think I can use it too. This is my hypothesis of spontaneous lip encounter: Without benefit of my brain, which was paralyzed in shock, my body decided that when my lips are kissed, I should kiss back. Cause and effect. Action and reaction. Touch fire, pull back. Windy day, reach for hairbrush. Squirrel in road, hit the brakes. Levi kisses me, kiss back.

See? It was a natural reaction, in essence, just a reflex.

So it didn't mean anything that I dug my fingers into his short hair or that when he went in with tongue, I felt a shudder rip through me like a 4.0 on the Richter scale, or that the kiss sort of morphed into a really long, extended mini make-out session.

Just reflexes. Normal stuff. Didn't mean a thing.

Obviously Levi thought so too, because when we broke for air, he looked at me, stunned. Sort of like my dad when he walked in and found the minivan through the kitchen wall.

"Uh . . ."

My thoughts exactly.

He should have left it at that. Instead, he had to be stupid enough to keep speaking. "Sorry, K. I didn't mean to do that."

With that, he turned and left the kitchen, leaving me standing there wondering why no one had given guys a manual. Like a *Things Not to Say to Girls Ever* kind of guidebook. Because what makes a guy think for one minute that any girl under any circumstances wants him to apologize for kissing her? It's like saying, "Sorry, but that was a total mistake. If I hadn't been temporarily insane due to testosterone, I would have never, ever kissed someone as (insert insulting adjective here) as you."

Apology = insult.

As I stood next to the kitchen island debating whether to let it drop or discuss the kiss further—not that I had any idea what to say about it other than ohmigod—the older construction guy nudged the younger one.

"Friendly family. Wish I was her brother."

Eew. I so wasn't having a good Saturday.

Chapter Two

Without making any eye contact with the pervy con-struction workers my parents had actually allowed into our house, I ran out of the room and up the stairs. I'd throw in the laundry that my mother had asked me to do first, then when someone else appeared in the kitchen, I'd finally get my cereal. There was no way I was setting foot back in there until another member of my family was present for protection.

I had mine and Zoe's laundry piled in a basket and was headed for Brandon's room to retrieve his and Levi's dirty clothes. I was trying not to feel weird about Levi—waaay too late for that—when it really hit me that Levi had kissed me. Okay, I mean I al-ready knew that, hence the initial freaking out, but it finally sank in what that actually meant. He had kissed me. Put his demon tongue in my mouth. I had kissed him back. Yet I had a boyfriend. Adam. Who I believe I've mentioned. More than once.

Boyfriend named Adam, demon named Levi kissing me—that pretty much meant I had cheated on my boyfriend, didn't it?

Didn't mean to do *that*. Yikes.

I bit my fingernails and knocked on Brandon's door and tried to rationalize my way around it. It hadn't been a premeditated kiss. It hadn't been initiated by me. Did that really make it cheating? Or just a sort of accidental meeting of the mouths?

Shouldn't there be like a five-second rule, anyway? Like dropping food on the floor. If you retrieve it immediately, you can still eat it. If the kiss lasted less than say, a minute, it didn't count. Right?

I thought about the way my toes had curled and my cheeks had flushed and I had leaned straight into Levi, my fingers in his hair.

Okay, who was I kidding? It was cheating. I couldn't deny it, because I had actually liked it. How disturbing was that?

Yet I really liked Adam. We were an odd couple, I'll admit, since he was Athlete and I was Artist, but it worked. We talked, we hung out, we giggled and kissed, and looked fab together holding hands.

Was I really going to ruin all that by snogging with a demon?

Brandon's door flung open and my brother glared at me, his hair sticking straight up. "What?"

My brother was fourteen and generally cranky and unhygienic. I don't know where he got that trait from. The unhygienic part that is. Cranky probably ran in the family.

"I need your laundry."

"It's in the closet." He moved to let me past, then peeled his T-shirt off of his head. "Take this one too." Swiping the shirt over his armpits, he held it out. "I've been sleeping in it for a week and it's getting ripe."

You think? I recoiled. "I'm not touching that. Just drop it in the basket."

He did, and it rolled off the pile and hit me in the chest. "Ugh." Using another shirt, I shoved it back onto the pile, then went to the closet and dumped their basket. I tried not to touch anything or think about the fact that I was staring at both my brother and Levi's dirty boxer shorts. That was just wrong on so many levels.

"Here's another one," Brandon said, holding up a white T-shirt. He put it to his nose and blew in it, the sound of snot releasing loud and revolting. Then he balled up the shirt and tossed it in my general direction.

I dodged it, my empty stomach churning with nausea. "You are completely disgusting."

"You're grounded," he said smugly.

And I was leaving. I left him and his snotty shirt to his disgusting devices and went down to the laundry room, grateful my mother was in the kitchen. She was a prosecuting attorney, so I did have some faith that she'd run a background check on the construction crew before she'd hired them, but that still didn't mean I wanted to be alone with them.

I threw the laundry in the washer, then poured my cereal before my mother could disappear and leave me defenseless. I started into the family room with my bowl.

"You can't eat in there!" she called after me.

"Why not?"

"The girls will be here in five minutes and I don't want any of them thinking they can eat in the family room."

"Fine." I started toward the stairs.

"Don't take that to your room! You'll leave the bowl for a week and then your room will smell like sour milk."

I paused, annoyed. I just wanted to be alone with my corn flakes. Was that too much to ask? The doorbell rang. Clearly it was.

"I'm eating in the van," I informed my mother, heading for the garage. "Zoe eats in there all the time," I added, to head off any arguments.

"Why can't you eat in the kitchen?" Mom asked, looking bewildered.

Because I didn't want creepy men staring at me while I chewed. Hello.

I didn't respond, just went for the car keys, and she was distracted by the doorbell ringing again.

"Whatever, just don't make a mess, Kenzie."

What was I, five? I could eat my cereal without incident, I was fairly confident. I grabbed a Diet Coke for good measure and skirted the creepy men to access the garage. At least sitting in the minivan I could see straight ahead into the kitchen and keep my eye on them. I wasn't sure why the workers were giving me that proceed-with-caution feeling—well, aside from the nasty brother comment—but they definitely were. Maybe it was just because I was in my pajama pants with bed head and it was early in the morning and they were in my kitchen. Or maybe my weird-ar (internal radar that goes off when weirdos are around) was giving me a warning and I should respect it.

After hitting the garage door to open it (just wanted privacy, not to kill myself with carbon monoxide), and climbing in to the driver's seat of the van, I spooned a mouthful of now soggy corn flakes into my mouth and chewed, staring at the hole I'd made with the front end of the minivan.

I wanted to be mad at Levi for entering my life, getting me grounded, then apologizing for kissing me, but it was hard to always stay mad at Levi. Most of the time I had to really work at it. I figured maybe I should think about that and why exactly that would be the case. Later. Like when I was in the nursing home. I'd have plenty of time to kick back in my footies in the lunch-room and think about it then.

At the moment, I really did not want to like him. He had kissed me, and when I should have ducked or leaped back or shoved him, I had rolled with it and now I was a big fat cheat who didn't deserve the cute smiley faces Adam texted me. I was feeling serious worry and self-disgust. I mean, did the rules of dating mean I had to come clean to Adam about it? And exactly just how would I feel if he had kissed another girl?

Pretty mean and ugly and hurt and sick to my gut, that's how I'd feel.

There had to be a way to blame this on Levi.

And I needed music.

Turning the van on, I adjusted the radio to a station that wasn't playing Disney music and gave myself a mental morals quiz.

1. Who would I be hurting by keeping the kiss a secret? No one.

2. Who would I be hurting if I told Adam? Both Adam and myself, which would be zero fun. We would break up, he would hate me, Levi would still be dating Amber Jansen, and I would be stuck sitting at home on Friday nights sticking pins in a voodoo doll of Levi, tortured, miserable, and wan. (Okay, slight exaggeration—I probably wouldn't go the voodoo doll route—but I'm just saying it wouldn't be good times.)

3. Omitting portions of the truth was still technically lying, which was wrong, but then again, wearing high-waisted jeans was wrong too, and people did that.

4. If someone dropped a twenty-dollar bill in front of me, I most definitely would give it back to them, which meant I was still a good person at my core.

Therefore, the logical conclusion was that the kiss had to be kept a secret. I was pretty sure. I really wished I could discuss the incident with my best friend Isabella, except she had an unexplainable crush on Levi, and she would not be objective or sympathetic to my problem. It would probably even further the space between us that had been growing huge lately because of Iz's resentment over my relationship with Adam. She was totally feeling left out, and I didn't want to make that worse, because I really missed her.

I pulled the soft drink can out of the pocket of my hoodie one-handed, juggling my cereal bowl with the other. My current kind of stress called for some serious carbonation. I leaned forward to hit the radio station again—not in the mood for Shakira, people—and popped the drink open.

And sprayed Diet Coke all over my legs, my hands, the dashboard, and on my corn flakes.

Whoops. Guess my internal anxiety actually shook up the can in my hoodie pocket. Or climbing in the van did it. One or the other. Licking my wrist to clean it off, I put the can down in the cup holder, rested the bowl on the floor between the seats, and glanced around for something absorbent. The radio was doing some weird in-and-out thing and I was starting to wonder if bubbly liquid pouring into its inner workings was enough to kill it. That would really thrill my father since he had spent time and money installing one of those satellite radio things.

Not to mention my mother's words about making a mess were rolling around in my head. I found old fast-food napkins in the glove compartment and was mopping at the dashboard with about zero success when I felt someone watching me. Looking up, I saw it was the dude in my kitchen, Brawny Boy. Just standing in the gaping hole of our kitchen wall and staring at me. Leering, actually. He met my eye, smiled, and waved.

I debated the best strategy. Blow him off, and it could either result in his leaving me alone or killing me while I slept. Wave back, and it could serve as unintentional encouragement or prevent me from a torturous death. I opted out of potential torture and gave him a lukewarm wave. I wasn't very brave in the face of deviance.

Slipping lower in the seat, I glared at the hole in the wall. I was not a demon slayer, no matter what Levi had said. I had closed the portal, but look what it had gotten me. I was condemned to eat soggy cereal in the van.

The door from the kitchen opened and I saw my mother. Zoe darted between her legs and ran into the garage. Realizing that the van smelled like milk, corn flakes, and Diet Coke, I hit the button to pop open the side door to air it out. My mom stepped out of the house and waved to someone other than me. I glanced back and saw some of the Girl Scouts plowing up the driveway and heading straight for the garage. I sighed. Privacy over. Time to play assistant to the stars. Zoe definitely was the Sutcliffe household star, which most of the time didn't really bother me. She was cute, smart, reasonably sweet, and stayed out of my bathroom.

At the moment, I could have done without the rabid curiosity she displayed on a regular basis. I could practically hear the heels of her black boots squealing as she hit the brakes on her way back to the kitchen. She had spotted me, and she leaned into the van, face filled with interest. "What are you doing in here?"

"Eating."

I was relieved to hear the radio had fixed itself. Not that I could actually tell what song was playing, because with no warning, Zoe, who had climbed into the van, let out a shriek, and her little friends immediately piled into the van behind her. They were a cluster of synthetic squealing five-year-olds, and they were going to step on my cereal bowl. "What the . . ." I had no idea what they were freaking out about and I couldn't see anything except for the seat and a mass of bodies crammed in a space too small for all of us.

"What on earth?" my mom said, stepping down into the garage.

Levi appeared in the doorway behind her. "What's up?"

"I have no idea," I said, about ready to open the driver side door and abandon them all. But if I left that bowl my mother would tack on an extra weekend to my punishment and that might send me over the edge.

"What do you have?" Mom asked them, leaning over the girls to investigate. "Good grief, there's a cat in the van! How the he— How in the world did that thing get in here?"

I loved it when my mother caught herself about to swear out loud, which was fairly often. I figured she had to keep the lid on so tightly with us kids, in particular Zoe, that when she was alone with my dad she probably dropped the "f" word like a rock star.

"The garage door was open," I said, finally catching a glimpse of a squirming cat through hot pink winter coats, bouncy pony-tails, and sparkly jeans. The cat was drinking the leftover milk in my bowl. Nice. "He must have wandered in. Don't pick him up, you guys, he might bite you or scratch you."

Too late. The petite blonde whose name I thought was Dakota already had the cat up in her arms, snuggled to her fake leopard fur coat. "It's just a kitten," she said.

Levi had leaned in, and he pulled Dakota—that was the name I was just going with because it seemed like it fit her—out into the garage, cat in tow. "It really is just a kitten, Mrs. S," he said. "Maybe six months old. And it doesn't have any tags."

The white ball of fluff was climbing up the fur of Dakota's coat and batting at her zipper pull.

"He's so cute!" Zoe said. "Can we keep him?"

"Well, we certainly can't throw him back out into the driveway," my mom said, with a heavy, heartfelt sigh like she really did just want to pitch the thing back out and pretend it had never appeared. Apparently her conscience wouldn't let her though, which was reassuring. "It's too cold. Bring him into the house, but after the meeting, we're going to try to find out if he has an owner."

Yeah, like that ever panned out. I decided we had just acquired a household pet, which actually might be cool, if I was ever allowed to get my hands on the cat. Chances were, Zoe would monopolize the poor thing, and I saw bonnets and baby carriage rides in the cat's future.

I reached for my cereal bowl as the girls all clamored out and into the kitchen. Levi opened the driver's door and waited for me.

He had a frown on his face.

"What's wrong?" I asked, glancing sadly at my soggy, warm, cat-licked cereal. I was still hungry.

"Kenzie."

Something about his tone made me forget about my complaining stomach. "What?" I had a feeling I wasn't going to want to hear whatever was about to come out of his mouth.

"Another demon portal just opened."

Yeah. Didn't want to hear that.

Chapter Three

"What is that supposed to mean?" I asked, even when I was pretty sure I knew exactly what it meant, and that the meaning sucked. Maybe if I played dumb or ignored it, the portal would just close all by itself and I could go back to simply stressing about losing Adam. Normal stuff. No more of this Kenzie vs. Creatures From Hell.

Levi leaned on the frame of the open door and eyeballed me like he was losing patience. "You know what it means. You closed the water portal. But now an air portal has opened. So you have to close it."

I glared at him. "Levi. It's the crack of freaking dawn on Saturday. I'm too tired to do anything more than brush my hair. *You* close the portal. Where is the portal, by the way?" I glanced around suspiciously, suddenly remembering that an open portal meant demon prisoners or prison guards could pop out at me unannounced at any given minute.

"I can't tell you."

See, this is where we had problems. Levi knew everything about demons and portals and prison but swore all the time that he couldn't tell me anything. That I had to figure it out myself. It's like when you're seven and you ask your mom what a stripper is and she tells you you'll understand when you're older. I was older. I still didn't get why women dance naked, and I still didn't know how I was supposed to close a new demon portal. And why did Levi and I have to play this game of paranormal charades all the time? What exactly was going to happen to him if he just straight out told me?

Maybe horrible demonic punishment for Levi would be forthcoming, but I was thinking we should just go for it and see what happened. I was tired of guessing and how bad could it really be, especially since it wouldn't be happening to me?

"Okay, so let's do a quick recap before I go into the house and get assaulted by craft materials," I said. "My house sits on a demon prison. My bathroom was one point in the pentagram that the prison forms, so when the portal opened up in my shower, you were able to escape. The other four points of the prison pentagram clearly are somewhere in the house as well, then, and if all five portals open, every prisoner in the demonic hellhole can escape. Is that right?"

"Yeah. That's the general idea."

"And according to you, only I can close the portals."

"You're also the only one who can open them."

Wait a minute. "You never told me that before."

"No?" He tried to look innocent and failed miserably.

"No." I narrowed my eyes. "What exactly am I doing to open them? I'll make sure I don't do it anymore."

He just shrugged. "You'll figure it out. Well, now that we're all caught up to speed, I'll head into the house."

The coward turned and went into the kitchen, leaving me once again alone in the minivan with my soggy cereal, my flat can of Diet Coke, and a view of the gaping hole in my kitchen wall.

Hello. *Gaping hole*. Created by me with the minivan. I was staring at the opened air portal, wasn't I?

And there was Brawny Boy again, standing there with his hammer in hand, just looking at me like he had nothing better in the whole wide world to do than just unnerve me. I debated going around and ringing the front doorbell rather than having to stroll past that freaky dude on my way into the kitchen.

Have I mentioned that I didn't want to be a demon slayer? That I just wanted to be an actress with a cute boyfriend? I wasn't brave. I wasn't aggressive. I was clumsy and a worrier and maybe just a little overdramatic. Sometimes. The thought of taking on demonic entities made me long for a milkshake and a fleece blanket for comfort.

Zoe's little face popped up in the hole. "Kenzie! Mom says you have to come in."

I went for it. Let the five-year-old protect me from the creepy construction worker.

Wait a minute. What if that guy was a demon? When I opened

the first portal in the shower, Levi popped out. If I had opened another portal in the kitchen wall, who was to say that another demon hadn't escaped? And was swinging a hammer. Nice.

Note to self: Ask Levi how to spot a demon at ten feet.

I grabbed the bowl and walked through the kitchen door. Zoe was far too close to that guy—potential demon—for my personal comfort. I set the bowl on the island, reached out, and picked her up, straining my arm muscles and just about ruining my back. Not exactly a heavyweight champ here, you know. I could barely open a soft drink can, and Zoe had grown when I wasn't looking.

But the gesture seemed to make her happy and she wrapped her legs around me and flung her arms around my neck.

"You have to see Marshmallow Pants," she said.

O-kay. "What is Marshmallow Pants?"

"Who," she corrected. "It's the kitten. I named him."

"Oh. Cool." I was sure that poor cat was just totally pumped to have a name that sounded like an emo band. "How did you come up with that name?"

"Because he's white and fluffy like a marshmallow and his butt looks like he's wearing pants."

Duh, me. It was all so very obvious. "Right."

I was carrying her out of the kitchen when she tapped the construction dude on the arm. "Hi," she said, when he turned.

"Hi," he answered, smiling first at Zoe, then at me.

Eye contact, bad. Didn't want to do that, and I couldn't believe that no one had taught the kid about stranger danger. Why was she chatting this guy up? Though it's probably dangerous to try to figure out where a five-year-old's actions are coming from, I figured that knowing Zoe, she was just showing off, trying to make sure she was the center of attention. Always. But I did not want her getting friendly with a potential demon. Okay, I realized she was pals with Levi, and that he lived in our house and everything, but he was *Levi*. He was annoying, but not evil. I didn't know anything about this guy and I wasn't taking any chances with my baby sister.

"Don't talk to him," I blurted, with zero tact.

"Why not?"

"He's working. You'll distract him and he'll cut off his thumb or something." There, that sounded less hysterical, more legitimate. Not like I thought he was a demon and he would know I thought he was a demon if he really was a demon.

"It's fine," he said, with another smile. "I'm Mike, by the way."

"I'm Zoe," my sister said with a queen's wave.

Forced to respond, I said, "Kenzie," then kept walking, straining under Zoe's weight. You know how you can feel someone's eyes watching you? Yeah. Felt Mike's. All the way to the family room. And they were freaking me out. If he was an escaped demon or a demon prison guard, Levi would tell me, right? For my protection and all. He would. I was almost sort of not really sure about it.

I set Zoe down on the sofa next to her pals, who were all industriously cutting something out of paper with scissors. Levi was sitting on the floor, his own project spread out on the carpet in front of him. Unbelievable. He was making a Halloween place mat, a ghost prominently featured in the center of his paper.

"Like it?" he asked me with a grin.

"Lovely."

Marshmallow Pants walked up and sat on Levi's half assembled place mat. "Hey, watch it," Levi said, staring the cat down. "You're wrinkling my art, dude." He tried to slide the cat over onto the carpet.

The oh-so-sweet and cute kitten calmly reached out and bit Levi on the hand.

"Hey! That was rude."

Probably. But funny. I leaned over and picked up some scraps of paper that were littering down to the floor from the couch to fulfill my helper duty obligations and possibly get sprung from my grounding sooner. Clearly I was putting a lot of effort into this. And clearly there was no chance of my parents suddenly feeling sorry for me and announcing an early end to grounding. I was stuck with the full term, so why work too hard?

Zoe jumped off the couch and scooped the cat up. "Marshmallow Pants is a baby. She doesn't know any better."

Did we know the cat was a girl? That was progress.

"Yeah, Levi, give the cat a break," I said. I scratched behind the cat's ears and got a loud purr.

Levi leaned forward and tried to do the same and got a big old hiss and bared teeth.

One of Zoe's friends, a big-eyed little brunette who shook like a Jell-O wiggler whenever she was excited, laughed and said, "I don't think Marshmallow Pants likes you, Levi."

That made two of us.

My whole day was ruined. I had cheated on Adam and now there was another portal open and Levi was all "can't tell you" about it. I wanted some ice cream to help me think but I couldn't even go into my kitchen because of Mike, possible demon, hanging around, strong and silent and somehow offensive. He was like body odor and I wanted him to go away.

I wanted everything to go away.

Except for Adam and his adoration for me.

That makes me sound a little less whiny, doesn't it?

Maybe not.

My mother, who was doling out glue sticks, said, "Levi, will you drop Kenzie off at the theater later? I need to go to the store and I'd appreciate it if you could drive her."

"Sure, Mrs. S. I'm happy to drive Kenzie wherever she needs to go." He gave a sweet and charming smile, just like the one on his driver's license. His fake driver's license that came from who knew where. A driver's license that allowed him to drive, whereas I had none, and therefore no ability to go anywhere, ever. After flunking my test (twice, but who's counting), I had driven the minivan through the kitchen with only my permit, and that meant no license until eighteen, which was a long wait.

It was a cruel, cruel world, all brought about by Levi, and maybe if I really was a demon slayer, I should just kill Levi too.

Online research was of no help whatsoever. I couldn't find any sites that gave step-by-step instructions on how a teenage demon slayer could close an open air portal. If I ever figured it out on my own, I was posting that info online, with sources sited, for other slayers to use. No one else should have to wade through mud the way I was.

I did a little pentagram research and got freaked out. And that was just reading the trigonometric values and the golden ratio descriptions and formulas. I had no idea I was actually going to stumble across math, my least favorite subject after Levi's driver's license.

Satanism was almost as scary as the math section. I read out loud, "The Hebrew name Leviathan is often inscribed in the pentagram."

Nice. That just happened to be Levi's full name, thank you very freaking much.

I sent him a text message.

Come to my room. Now.

I knew he was somewhere in the house, but I was too busy staring at pictures of goats impaled with pentagrams to bother getting up and finding him. Who knew goats could look so evil? I'd never look at cheese the same way again.

Grabbing a notebook out of my desk drawer, I flipped it open to a clean piece of paper and drew a really lame aerial of my house, roof off. I was thinking that if the bathroom was the tip of the pentagram, I really should figure out where all five portals were supposed to be.

On another piece of paper, I drew a pentagram and cut it out. No place mat crafts for me, thank you very much. I was building a model of the top of the demonic correctional facility for demons of envy. Just a typical Saturday.

Spinning the paper around to align the tip with my bathroom, I didn't like what I saw.

Levi appeared in my doorway, hands in his front pockets. "Are you flirting with me?" he asked. "Because if you are, I have to warn you, your mom is still downstairs."

That earned him an eye roll. "Hardly. If I was flirting, which I wouldn't be, I would be more charming."

"Would you?" He made like that totally surprised him.

I was annoyed but decided to drop it in the interest of conducting business and getting him out of my room faster. "Look at this. If I'm looking at this right, then the points of the pentagram are my bathroom, the kitchen, Zoe's room, my parent's room, and the family room. A portal in Zoe's room is not cool, Levi."

"Well, no worries." Levi took the paper with the pentagram and spun it. "You have to have the two tips pointing northward, and the other three down toward hell, where the fallen angels live. That means Zoe's room does not have a portal in it, so it's all good."

"All good" was pushing it, but I was relieved. I didn't want Zoe possessed by a demon. She already had her moments of Satanism.

"So that means the bathroom and the kitchen," I said, studying the paper. "Maybe the family room . . . it's kind of hard to tell on that one. Brandon's room, which is okay, I guess, since you're staying there. And . . ." I stopped talking. Squinted. Tried to maneuver the paper a little.

"Your room," Levi said cheerfully. "That makes sense."

Yikes. My room? I didn't want my baby sister possessed, but I didn't want some demon popping out of my closet while I was sleeping either. "Why does that make sense?"

"Because—" Levi cleared his throat and spun the paper around. For an otherworldly creature, he sucked at lying. "You know, because that's the way the pentagram works."

"What are you not telling me?" I snatched the paper out of his hand and set it down next to my Hello Kitty mouse pad. "I could use a little help here."

"Nothing. I've told you everything I can."

There was the problem. *Can* was that little tag on the end of his sentence that meant I knew squat and he wasn't going to enlighten me anytime soon.

His cell phone buzzed in his pocket. He pulled it out to check a text message.

I wasn't going to ask. Wasn't going to ask . . .

"Who was that?" Curiosity killed the cat and Kenzie Sutcliffe. I couldn't help myself.

"Amber."

Of course it was Amber. His girlfriend. Homecoming queen to his king. Head cheerleader. Ruler of all things pink and gold. Rich, pretty, owned a car to go along with her license . . . Need I go on?

Not that I cared. "Tell her I said hi."

"Sure."

The way he said it told me he wasn't going to say anything to

Amber about me at all, and the truth was, why would he? Amber could care less whether or not I greeted her, which just showed I had better manners. She made me feel petty and jealous and disgusted with myself for feeling same said pettiness and jealousy, but at least I could put that aside and say hello. Point for Kenzie's maturity.

Levi laughed at something Amber had texted him while I stared at my computer screen, the points of the pentagram blurring together.

"She's at the soccer game."

I sat up straight. "What soccer game?"

"The traveling team Adam's on. They're playing in Hampton Heights."

I knew exactly where they were playing because Adam had asked me to come to the game, but I had to say no due to my grounding and my afternoon voice lessons at the theater. "Why is Amber there?"

"Because a lot of our friends are on the team." He wasn't looking at me, but was staring at his phone while his fingers moved lightning speed.

"Why aren't you there?"

Levi glanced up and smiled. "I'm keeping you company."

I wanted to believe him, I really did. But I couldn't help but be suspicious. Given that Levi always had a goal, I couldn't help but think he wasn't just hanging out with me out of the kindness of his demonic heart.

"Why don't you try out for the traveling team?" Levi was a newfound star on the West Shore High soccer team. He could defy the laws of gravity with his hang time in the air.

"Those private teams are seriously expensive. I don't have any money." He shrugged, like it didn't matter.

"Oh." I had never thought about the fact that Levi had no income. He seemed to have a decent collection of clothes, a cell phone, an iPod. I guess I'd never bothered to wonder where his spending money came from. It seemed rude to ask him. But when had that ever stopped me with Levi?

"Where do you get *any* money?"

"Demon bank. But I can only withdraw limited funds." Levi didn't sound particularly interested in the conversation, his fingers still moving on his cell. "Hey, Amber says Adam just scored a goal. She's cheering for him."

That made me forget all about money and the bizarreness of a demon bank, which sounded way too like a sperm bank for my personal comfort. Amber's cheering for Adam—what did that mean exactly? I felt a nervous sweat breaking out in gross places. I was at home with Levi and we had kissed. Amber was at the soccer game with Adam, cheering him on. That was all sorts of wrong. We needed to do a little body shuffling and get everything back on track. To normal. Levi and Amber, Kenzie and Adam. That was the way it was supposed to be. I was never all that thrilled about Levi hooking up with Amber, but if Amber was with Levi, then Amber couldn't be making the moves on my Adam.

So I blurted out, "Don't tell Amber you kissed me."

That got his attention. He looked up at me, astonished. "Why the hell would I tell her that?"

"I don't know. But just don't. Ever. For any reason." I slapped my hand on the desk, just in case it wasn't totally clear that I was saying *Don't do it.*

"Yeah, like I'm totally stupid. Please. I'm not going to say anything. And it was a mutual thing, by the way."

"What do you mean?" I chewed the pink tips of my dark hair, worried. Bad enough if Adam found out from me, but if Amber told him? Ugh. That scene was too nauseating to think about.

"We kissed each other," Levi clarified. "I didn't kiss you."

Excuse me? "Yes, you did!" I was there. I remembered with total clarity his head bending down and his lips landing on mine first.

"We both wanted it," he said stubbornly.

Wanted it? Wanted it? Only after he forced it on me. And that was only because I was caught off guard and my brain had actually probably thought it was Adam kissing me for the first thirty seconds, and then by the point of recognition my body was confused and responding purely physically.

"Whatever, Levi. If you're not going to tell me how to close this stupid portal, just get out of my room." Before I threw a pentagram at him.

Chapter Four

Levi was singing "Sexy Back" at the top of his lungs as he drove me to the theater in my mom's minivan. I was searching for some way to stab out my eardrums so I wouldn't have to hear his screeching anymore when I noticed flashing lights in the rearview mirror.

"How fast are you driving?" We were on the highway and that was definitely a cop behind us, signaling for Levi to pull over.

"Uh . . . Eighty-five."

"That's twenty miles over the speed limit. You're going to get a ticket." Was that glee in my voice? Oh, yeah. Most definitely.

Levi turned the radio down and glanced in the mirror. "I've never gotten a ticket and I've been driving for decades."

Sometimes I had a hard time processing that Levi was half a millennium old, given his maturity was close to that of a baby baboon. He had explained to me that his memories faded with time, leaving him with mostly short-term memories (short term being relative in demon speak) and a frozen maturity. He really was sixteen for all practical purposes. But sometimes when he pointed out his age, it was mildly—okay, severely—disturbing.

As was the fact that he'd been driving for decades and I wasn't even allowed to swing up to the high school or Target because of the car-through-the-kitchen incident.

"Well, you're going to get one now. Guess you'll be dropping by the demon bank for a withdrawal because you're looking at a hundred-dollar ticket."

"You don't have to sound so excited about it." Levi had pulled over onto the side of the highway and parked the van. He checked his seatbelt, ran his fingers through his short brown hair, and waited for the cop.

"Cops make me anxious," I said.

"Yeah, you sound really worried."

Busted. I grinned at him.

The police came over and indicated for Levi to open his window. Levi smiled politely and said, "Is there a problem?"

"You were doing eighty-five in a sixty-five. I need your license."

"Sorry. I'll be more careful. My girlfriend"—Levi gestured to me—"is late to a class and she's harping at me. She told me to go faster."

Gasp. The loser had just dragged me into his speeding ticket. I was blustering too much to say anything in protest, but the cop glared at me.

"You should know better than that. Leave the house earlier next time." Then he said to Levi with a stern reprimand, "You going to jump off a bridge if she tells you to? Get a backbone, kid. Girls will always drag you into trouble if you let them."

What kind of a blanket sexist statement was that? Like the history of humanity proved that it was girls stirring the pot? I don't think so. If anyone was getting anyone in trouble it was the opposite—boys dragging girls down. War. Corsets. High heels. Panty hose. The perming rods of the eighties. All created by men. Not that I knew any of that for a fact, but it had to be true. Why else would women have put fuzzy ringlets in their hair?

Not that I was going to argue with a police officer, me who didn't even have a license and who was already severely grounded. Wasn't going to touch that one, so I just clamped my lips shut and squeezed my purse in my lap.

"Okay," Levi said, and handed him his license. When the cop walked back to his car to run the license Levi grinned at me. "No ticket. Watch and writhe in envy."

"Why? Are you hungry?" Levi had a charming little demon characteristic. He fed on other people's envy. It worked for him like pizza for me—it made him feel full and happy. I tried hard not to be the one generating his after-school envy snack, but there were times when I failed, and when he wasn't sucking sustenance off of me, there were plenty of people in school who had envy Levi could engorge on. We lived in the suburbs, land of I Want One. He was definitely never going to starve.

"I could use a little something."

The policeman came back and handed Levi his license. "Alright, I'm going to let it slide this time with a warning. But slow it down, speed demon."

Then he was gone and I was left gaping at Levi. "What happened here?"

"Just my amazing charm and powers of persuasion."

"You used your demon mojo to influence him, didn't you?" How wrong was that? And why didn't I have that kind of power?

"Uh, yeah. What good is having it if I don't take advantage of it?" Levi said with really irritating logic as he glanced in the mirror and sped up to pull back onto the highway.

"Okay, I admit it. I'm totally jealous. Eat up." I leaned against the window, the glass cooling my hot forehead. I felt tired.

"What's the matter, K?"

"Nothing." There was, but I couldn't exactly pinpoint what it was. Probably worry over Adam, which I could not discuss with Levi. Fear, maybe, that I couldn't close another portal when taking out the first one had gotten me in such serious trouble. And irritation that I was chronically dependent on the chauffeuring skills of my demonic companion.

"Come on, what's wrong?"

"Nothing."

"Tell me."

"Nothing."

"I don't believe you. Just spill it."

"It's nothing," I said, getting exasperated.

"We can do this the whole way to the theater. It's still ten minutes away. Or you can just tell me."

"There's nothing to tell." I gritted my teeth and glared at him.

"Yes, there is. I know you. You're upset about something."

"Maybe I'm just moody."

"Well, I know *that*."

Hey. Totally untrue. "I'm not moody!"

"So then what's wrong?"

Do you see why I frequently wanted to go into a dark closet and scream repeatedly?

I hit on the one way I could get him to drop it. "I have PMS . . . really bad cramps." I didn't, but that subject was guaranteed to get a teenage male to zip his flapping lips.

"Oh." His tone totally changed from encouraging to horrified. "Sorry."

He was silent for a second, changing lanes on the highway, while I enjoyed my triumph in getting him to shut up. Then he said, "Did you take some ibuprofen? That should help. We can stop at the drugstore if you haven't and buy some."

Have I mentioned Levi made it really hard to hate him sometimes?

Isabella sipped from her water bottle and eyed me. "What's the matter with you?"

"Nothing. Why does everyone think something is wrong with me today? I'm just tired."

"Meow. Relax. I was just asking. You know, out of concern, seeing as you're my best friend."

Setting her water down, Isabella did some really amazing leg kicks to keep her muscles loose. She was a dancer and was taking a break between her two Saturday classes, Advanced Ballet and Workout for the Dancer's Body. Both required a skill level and balance that I didn't possess, though I had taken tons of ballet, jazz, and dance for the theater in an attempt to gain chorus parts in productions. Isabella wanted to be a professional dancer, but given my average skills at the barre, I was pinning my hopes on my acting skills in my post–high school New York City life.

Not that my parents knew I was planning to ditch Ohio for the Big Apple. That little surprise would have to wait until after I got a nice big juicy graduation present. Then we could have that battle out.

"I'm sorry," I said, knowing I sounded bratty. "It's just exhausting to be grounded. And Levi is driving me crazy, as usual." Though how crazy I couldn't share. Iz didn't know about the whole demon thing, and that was starting to unnerve me. It was this huge mega-major secret that only Levi and I knew, and it felt so totally wrong not to be able to talk about it with the person I had shared everything else with since the age of ten.

"I don't understand why the two of you don't get along. He's so sweet. And cute."

Isabella bent over to stretch her eight-mile-long legs again, her raven black hair neatly up in a bun, her black leotard lint-free and flattering. Isabella was Grace, I was Goofball. It worked for us.

Even if she had somehow fallen under the Levi Influence. "We don't get along because I have no boy-girl feelings for him"—liar, liar—"and when you take that element away, he's hard to deal with."

"It's probably because your mothers are good friends and you grew up with that whole 'we're cousins' thing."

That was a lie Levi had told everyone, and it was hard to keep feeding it to my best friend, so I didn't say anything.

She didn't seem to notice and asked, "How are things with Levi and Amber? They break up yet?"

That was Isabella's hope and dream—that Levi and Amber would spontaneously combust and then Isabella could swoop in and show him that his true happiness lay in taking her out on Friday nights. I had no good news for her and this ill-fated lie-in-wait plan.

"They seem fine. I'm sorry, Iz."

She frowned but seemed resigned. "I do have an idea though. We need to have a Halloween party at your house, and we'll invite a bunch of people, including Levi, but not Amber."

"Won't he just bring her? I mean when you invite someone they kind of just bring their girlfriend or boyfriend along, like an appendage. You can't really leave your arm at home."

"She is not his arm," Isabella said in disdain. "There is nothing about her he needs."

Amber didn't seem to know that, because she totally acted like he needed her every second of every day.

"We'll plan the party for the night of the football game, and then she can't come," Isabella said.

"Then Adam won't be able to come either." My boyfriend, at least my boyfriend until he learned I was a disgusting cheat (not that he would because I wasn't going to tell him and it was all going to be fine), was a placekicker for the football team since he had brilliant foot moves from soccer.

She made an exasperated sound. "Well, I don't know. We'll figure something out. But the point is, we'll get Levi there, no Amber, and then I'll get him alone and convince him he needs to be with me."

There seemed to be some holes in that plan.

And I wasn't pointing them out.

Because even if I thought the plan wasn't really a plan but just sort of grasping at anything that might somehow, if all the planets aligned, result in Isabella and Levi's getting together, I wasn't going to take that hope away from her. She hadn't done that to me, back when I was seriously crushing on Adam, and he was not even looking at me in Anatomy and Physiology class, let alone talking to me or indicating in any way I was of more importance than the chair he sat on. Actually, the chair had probably been more important, because it was useful, and at that point, I was pretty much irrelevant in Adam's life.

Or so I had thought. And so Isabella had thought. But the point was, she never told me that. She indulged my crush, encouraged me to not sit back, to go for it and see what might happen, and here I was, together with Adam in a brand new budding relationship.

I had to do the same for her, even if I thought she and Levi were about as likely a couple as . . . salt and pepper? No, they went together. There was one of those mom metaphors about food that I was trying to think of but couldn't, but you get the point. Two things that didn't belong together. Isabella and Levi were a mismatch.

But I had to support Isabella even if Levi had a girlfriend.

Even if he had kissed me.

"Okay," I said, thrusting my guilt to the back of my brain. "We'd better pick the date and start inviting people. I don't know if we should do a Halloween theme though since Halloween is actually tomorrow. We'll have to plan the party for next weekend."

"No! That's it. We'll have the party tomorrow night, on Halloween. And people will think it's seriously cool to have a party on a Sunday and to get a last-minute invite. It's very Hollywood. And we can just not invite Amber."

She looked thrilled and I could tell she was creating a mental invite list.

Me? Not so thrilled. I wasn't exactly sure how I was going to convince my parents that even though I was grounded, I really should be allowed to have a spontaneous Halloween party on a school night solely for the purpose of breaking up Levi and Amber. Not that I intended to do anything to break the happy couple up. I didn't like Amber, but there wasn't a vengeful or malicious bone in my body. I just couldn't stomach the idea of inserting myself between two people. Intentionally, that is. I bit my lip when I realized in a way, I had done just that, and it was seriously not a good thing, and could I feel any crappier? But while I wasn't going to break them up—not on purpose, anyway—I wasn't going to disillusion Isabella either, and who knows? If Levi and Amber had a massive fight and split, maybe Levi would actually *want* to be with Isabella despite the fact that they had absolutely nothing in common. There was no predicting these things. I hadn't seen a demon popping out of my shower coming and that had happened. I had no idea what Isabella saw in Levi (okay, lying again), but who was to say they weren't made for each other?

It was all so complicated and I needed sugar. There was unfortunately none to be found in the hallway at the theater.

But as for my parents, they were likely, just based on knowing my parents, going to laugh hysterically at all our party logic and tell me no way.

So I'd have to do some maneuvering, because Isabella really wanted the party and I had been feeling bad that we weren't spending as much time together as we had pre-Adam. And then there was the guilt over Levi and his lips on mine, which was getting worse by the minute.

"Okay, we need to get Levi to ask my parents about the party. They'll tell me no, but they'll let him do it." If not, he could throw some of that famed demon mojo on them and convince them to say yes.

"Should we say costumes are required?"

"It's a Halloween party. Of course." I smiled at her.

Letting loose all our friends under a shroud of fake spider-webs had the potential to be a lot of fun.

Agreeing to a party on twenty-four hours' notice to make Isabella feel better was fine in theory. Actually putting that plan into motion was a different story.

The minute Isabella had walked away with a cheerful wave to go back to dance class, I had started stressing. Levi wasn't answering his phone and he was crucial to the success of Halloween Happiness.

When Adam picked me up to go home, I was biting my nails. We were going back to my house to watch a movie, my parent's compromise to the grounding. I could have Adam over for two hours, no more, and we couldn't actually go anywhere. Which seriously decreased our ability to make out, which seriously sucked.

But they could have been totally evil and not let me see him at all, so I wasn't going to whine. Too much.

"What's the matter?" Adam said a minute after I climbed into his SUV.

"Nothing." What could I say? I'm worried that the demon who lives with me who appeared in my shower and is dating Amber isn't answering his cell phone so I can make him force my parents to allow a party on zero notice so that same said demon can be lured into a romantic relationship that he didn't know he wanted with my best friend?

Adam might actually consider that a little strange.

"Are you sure you're okay? You look worried." Which made Adam look worried. And Adam worried was even cuter than Adam not worried.

I leaned my head on his shoulder for a brief second since he was actually pulling out of the parking lot and I didn't want to cause an accident. But it was nice to lean on him. He was tall, with black hair, perfect teeth, a rock-solid body (all those sports were boring to watch, but they did lovely things to his build), and a very sweet smile. Adam made me feel safe, protected, and not at all self-conscious, which was funny because for months I had secretly liked him, and had spent every day sitting next to him in science class sweating through my hoodies in uncomfortable silence hoping he'd notice me.

Now that he had noticed me and asked me to Homecoming, even though we'd only been together a few weeks, it was easy to be with Adam. He didn't make stupid guy jokes, he didn't try to maul me every chance he got, and he didn't forget to call me back. He was thoughtful, fun to talk to, and probably not as smart as me (had to admit that helped my feelings of security), but not dumb to the point where I wanted to knock on his skull.

Nothing about Adam annoyed me, really, which was more than could be said for some people.

Like people whose names started with L and ended with i. And had an ev in the middle.

"I'm fine. Just tired. They started work on the kitchen this morning and my mom was bitter that it screwed up her morning coffee routine. She made me get up and help with Zoe's Girl Scout thing." Speaking of my mother, I pulled my phone out and texted Levi to call me. He really needed to ask my mom about this party.

"Who are you texting?" Adam asked, glancing over at me, his baseball hat shadowing his eyes. "Isabella?"

"No. Levi. Isabella wants to have a Halloween party at my house. Tomorrow. And I told her Levi was going to have to ask my parents because they will never let me do it. They'll let him do it, though, which is seriously irritating."

"When is he moving back in with his parents?" Adam asked, oh-so-casual.

"I don't know. They're getting divorced and they hate each other, and they're both refusing to move out of the house, so they're like throwing knives at each other and crap, so they don't want him there right now." That was the story Levi had told everyone, anyway, even though as far as I could tell, he had no parents. Yet he had even managed to produce a woman on the phone to discuss the whole fake sordid situation with my mom so she would agree to let him live with us.

"That sucks."

I wasn't sure what Adam meant sucked exactly, but I thought he meant pretty much everything about it, including that Levi, who was not related to me, lived in my house, three feet down the hallway.

Or maybe that was just my guilt laying suspicion at Adam's feet.

My stomach suddenly hurt. "Totally," I agreed, massaging my gut.

Could guilt actually eat through stomach lining in half a day?

"I think Levi likes you," Adam added, straight out of nowhere.

Yikes. I played dumb. "As a friend, yeah, we get along. We kind of have to, living in the same house. And you know, our moms are good friends and everything."

"No, I mean he *likes* you likes you. Like he wants you to play secretary to his boss."

It was a good thing I wasn't drinking anything because I would have spewed it all over Adam's windshield.

"*What?*" I squeaked, majorly, seriously, catastrophically grossed out by that phrasing Adam had so casually thrown out there. "What are you talking about? He so doesn't!"

"He totally does."

"I . . . I . . ." What was I trying to say? I had lost command of the English language in my horror. "Nuh-uh."

That was really putting some conviction behind it. "He's with Amber anyway."

"I'm just saying," Adam said.

"What? What are you saying?"

"That he likes you."

"No, he doesn't!" And the thing was, I wasn't even really lying. I didn't think Levi liked me that way. I thought he was totally telling the truth when he had said he hadn't meant to kiss me. Not very flattering, but I did think it was just that Levi had been close to me and he had kissed me on total impulse. No big thing.

"I think it might surprise you how much he's into you."

Adam had clearly made his decision and nothing I said was going to convince him otherwise. "What does it matter anyway? I'm positive he doesn't, but so what if he did? I don't like him. At all."

"I'm just saying," Adam repeated.

Saying what? God. I had that go into a closet and scream feeling again. I was surrounded by obtuse men. And neither one probably even knew what obtuse meant. Maybe I didn't either, now that I thought about it.

Did I even really know *anything*?

"Can we stop by here?" I pointed to the United Dairy Farmers store. "I want some ice cream."

Sugar and cream always made everything better.

It was a rule.

Chapter Five

I got three texts and a phone call from Levi while Adam and I were cuddled up on the couch watching a movie that made Adam laugh and left me confused. I would never understand why bodily functions were considered so funny by guys. But Adam was amused for the most part, until my phone rang. Levi's ring tone, which was the music from the movie *Halloween*, was jarring and creepy.

"Is he calling you again?" Adam asked, glaring at my phone as I went to scoop it up off the coffee table.

"It's the first time he's called me. We're trying to figure out this whole Halloween party thing."

I answered it, which I knew wouldn't make Adam happy, but I also knew Levi. He would keep texting or calling until I answered, and I had texted him first. In all fairness to him, he would actually worry about me if he didn't hear back from me. So I said, "Hello. How are you?"

"Fine. What do you need me for?"

"You have to"—I glanced around to make sure my mother wasn't in earshot—"tell my mom you want to have a couple of friends over tomorrow night for Halloween. That you'll help pass out candy and stuff."

"What friends am I having over?" he asked suspiciously.

"Everyone on the list I give you. It's only fifteen people."

"So it's a party."

"Sort of." I bit my fingernail. "Look, my mom will tell me no, but she'll let you do it. Please?"

It seemed weird that I was basically begging him to have a party that would actually ensure his and Isabella's future happiness—something I suspected had never even occurred to him. The whole plan was starting to feel a little, well, stupid. But I was in now and couldn't back out. Isabella would never forgive me, and I'd already annoyed Adam. I had to just roll with it.

"Kenzie. This isn't a good idea."

"Probably not," I agreed. "But just do it, Levi."

"You know I'd do anything for you."

"Well, if you'll do anything for me, then in comparison this is totally easy. It's just saying you're having a few friends over. No biggie."

Levi sighed. "Fine. I'll talk to your mom tonight. I'll be home in an hour."

"Yay. Thank you."

"By the way, am I on the invite list?"

"Of course. You have to be there or my mom will catch on."

"Is Adam?"

"Of course."

"Can I bring Amber?"

"It would be better if you didn't," I said cheerfully, glad he'd asked me outright. "She wants to scratch my eyes out and it kind of drags the room down."

Another sigh. "Fine."

"Thanks! I'll see you later." And I hung up before he could ask any further questions.

Adam stared at me, his long legs, which had been so close to mine, suddenly pulled to the left about a mile away. "He said he'll do anything for you?"

"Umm. Yeah." I bit my lip and tried to look innocent and casual. "Cuz we're friends." Who had shared one teeny, tiny, measly kiss.

"If you say so," Adam said, turning back to the TV, his expression gloomy.

I was starting to figure out it was totally impossible to make all people happy at once. Maybe that was obvious, and we all knew it, but it was still worth noting that it sucked.

Kenzie Sutcliffe + Impulsiveness = Disaster.

Yeah. Planning a party that is not supposed to appear to actually be a party that is intended to alter the course of your best friend's life with about a minute to work through the details? That is not a plan. That is reckless optimism.

My mom had said yes to Levi's request to have some friends over, and so to make it seem legit in her eyes (and not my trying to wiggle around being grounded, which, hello, I so was) we decided to invite mostly West Shore soccer players and their girlfriends. And guess what? Adam was a West Shore soccer player. And I was his girlfriend. Wow. Were we brilliant or what? We figured my mom wouldn't think anything of Isabella's being there, since she was always at our house, even if she wasn't attached to a soccer player.

Having Dirk Danger there (yes, that was really his name, proving that parents do have a sense of humor) didn't thrill me since he had morphed into Levi's Mini-Me, but Levi wouldn't invite friends over without him, so we were stuck with Dirk and his inability to use cologne without dumping the entire contents of the bottle on himself. Being around Dirk was like entering the pig barn at the county fair—you just held your nose and breathed through your mouth until you got lightheaded and made an excuse to leave the room. If you were lucky Dirk took his Pig-Pen cloud of Ralph Lauren four feet or more away from you before you saw spots from a blinding chemical headache.

Otherwise, I was cool with the guest list. Adam and his friends, Reggie and Justin, plus Justin's girlfriend, Darla, and her friend Madison. Two other soccer players whose positions on the field I could never remember—but were the kind who run up and down between the goals a lot—and their girlfriends rounded out the crowd. Dirk didn't have a girlfriend (imagine that), and he threw off our even number of guys and girls, so Levi had invited Cecily Thrombauck, who had significant enough asthma that Dirk's cologne probably couldn't penetrate her lungs and kill her the way it did the rest of us.

You're with me so far, right? It all made sense. We'd thought it through.

What I didn't realize is that asking humans to put on costumes says a lot about who they are, what they think of themselves, and what they find funny—things sometimes you're just better off not knowing. Levi was no exception.

When he came down the stairs dressed all in black with a ton of pictures of women Velcroed all over his chest, back, and legs, I just stared at him. "What are you supposed to be? And is that the Olsen twins stuck to your gut?"

I probably shouldn't have asked, because he stuck out his arms, grinned, and said, "I'm a chick magnet."

Oh my God. "I think I just vomited in my mouth."

Levi just laughed. "What are you?"

I was wearing a blue trapeze dress, devil horns, and a devil tail. To avoid clashing, I had quickly dyed the tips of my hair back to red instead of pink, and I thought it was a good effect. "Hello. I'm a devil with a blue dress on." It was obvious.

"Your horns don't look real," he said dismissively, going for the front door as the doorbell rang. "But you are pure evil when you're in a bad mood."

"They're not supposed to look real!" I yelled after him. "It's iconic."

He didn't care. And he sucked some of the pride in my costume away, which ticked me off.

As I set out munchies, Justin and Darla strolled into the family room. I wasn't entirely sure what their costumes were supposed to be, but they looked very . . . plastic. Lots of makeup on
Darla, high pink pumps, a blond wig. Justin had a tight sweater
on with a big *K* on the front. "Uhhh . . ." I said.

"We're Barbie and Ken," Darla told me.

Nice. I laughed. "That's hilarious. Where's your Corvette?"
And how whipped was Justin that he let Darla talk him into being
Ken? I thought it said good things for the future of their rela-
tionship, and I totally liked a guy who had a sense of humor.

Justin was grinning and chasing after Darla, hands out ready
to grope, saying in a fake deep voice, "Come on, Barbie, let's go
party."

"Oh, Ken," Darla said, falsetto, with a giggle as she ran
around the table in her heels to escape Justin. "I'm having such a
good time."

Stop me if I ever try to wear a Barbie costume. I can't pull off
perky like that.

Reggie and Madison came in two minutes later dressed like a
dish and a spoon. Interesting choice for two people who swore
up, down, and sideways that they were just friends. Not that din-
nerware was sexy or anything, but in the nursery rhyme the dish
ran away with the spoon, and it was obvious it wasn't to go to the
grocery store. But I wasn't going to say anything. Let them live in
Deluded Land together. As a dish and a spoon.

60

"You're a present?" I asked Dirk, when he strolled in wrapped up in gift wrap and a bow, his cologne cloud still intact despite the fact that he was wearing a cardboard box. "Way to be modest."

"Did you see my gift tag?" he asked with a smirk, turning so I could see the big tag on his shoulder.

"To: Women. From: God." He was not saying . . .

"Get it? I'm God's gift to women."

Snort. On what planet? "You are totally delusional. But it is funny, I'll give you that."

Cecily arrived as a bee and I shoved her in Dirk's direction. Everyone was there except for Adam and Isabella and I was starting to wonder if somehow Adam had forgotten to mention that he was dumping me, when he finally showed up. Wearing a gladiator costume.

Oh. My. God. He looked so hot that I needed a lobster bib for my drool. The beauty of an athletic boyfriend was that he wasn't scrawny or chunky. He was firm, and muscular, and filled out in all the right places, and he was man enough to stroll in wearing a freakin' skirt. I must have passed out from overwhelming admiration because the next two minutes don't actually exist in my memory.

If I had to guess I would say I sweated and giggled and made no sense, but if that did happen, I was glad I didn't remember it. I do know I stared at him as if I were having an out-of-body experience, time frozen to a halt as I checked him out head to toe, focusing in particular on his eyes, lips, legs, biceps, hair, jaw, butt . . . Okay, I was focusing on everything, which was probably why I forgot to breathe until he squeezed my hand.

"Hey, Kenzie. You look adorable," he murmured to me.

Adam murmured really well. It was like fingers walking up and down my back.

"Thanks. You look hot," I said, because I didn't do subtle.

Adam laughed. "I figured if Brad Pitt, Russell Crowe, and Colin whatever his name is could pull it off, why can't I?"

"You can," I assured him. Yay me for having a hot boyfriend.

I would be such a loser moron if I screwed that up and I just wasn't going to.

We were eating chips, talking, listening to creepy mood music, and letting Zoe parade through the family room ten times as each phase of her angel costume was put into place, while I wondered where Isabella was. I texted her three times and got no answer as the clock ticked toward six. Trick-or-treaters were going to be ringing the bell any minute. Levi was making some serious headway into a bowl of trail mix when Isabella opened the front door and walked in, shedding her coat.

Levi choked on a nut, coughing it back into his hand, his face turning red. "Isabella?" he asked, voice laced with shock.

I understood the feeling. My best friend had lost her mind. She was wearing a bikini top, bikini bottoms, and filmy chiffon pants that vaguely pretended to cover her legs but let you see everything. She had failed to share with me that she was going to dress as the Slutty Genie.

She looked completely nonchalant and gave him a smile. "Hey, Levi. What's up?"

My Mary Janes clicking on the hardwood floor, I marched over to her and headed her off in the entryway. "What are you wearing? And why are you so late?"

"I'm Jasmine," she said with a frown. "The Disney princess. See?" She pointed to the headband she was wearing over her black hair.

"Iz. I realize Jasmine showed her stomach, but she was only a cartoon. You're like an inch from naked."

"It's a costume. Besides, I look good in it. Why is that a big deal?"

Help. Where was I supposed to go with that? "I just don't think that you need to take it all off to impress Levi. He's not like that."

"I'm not taking it all off. Give me some credit, God. It's just a costume."

"A nonexistent costume."

Isabella glared at me. "What is your problem? Now that you're with Adam you get to be the morality police? I've worn less than this on stage in productions and recitals, so chill out."

I found that seriously hard to believe, but I let it go. "So why are you late?"

"I had to wait until my mom left to put this costume on. She'd freak out if she saw me wearing this."

Hello. You would think that would clue her in that maybe it

was over the top, but then again, when did any of us think our mothers were in any way reliable about evaluating our clothes? Iz's mom wore appliquéd sweatshirts with horse heads on them, and I always thought that was probably where the phrase "take the horse out back and put it down" came from. Those sweatshirts needed to be shot and killed.

I was debating saying something else when Zoe came back into the room, her halo bouncing. She was holding a big fluff of white in her arms as she came over to Isabella and me. "Look at Marshmallow Pants! He's an angel too."

Wow. He was. And I noticed that the cat, which had been a she the day before, was now a he. Who knew what its gender really was, but it was definitely an angel, no doubt about it. There was lots of white satin, tulle, and gold trim. The feather halo strapped onto the cat's head and secured under his chin was a nice touch.

I couldn't believe my mother had actually let Zoe talk her into buying a pet angel costume for the cat. That was crazy. My mom didn't do cutesy, nor did she waste a dime when she didn't have to. But somehow she had agreed to the über-precious costume for the cat, who clearly didn't appreciate the beauty of his current appearance. Angry black eyes blinked up at me and I almost felt sorry for the little smoosh-faced critter.

Levi didn't seem to feel bad for it at all. He had wandered over and was laughing loudly. "Dude. No way." He reached out and made the halo wave back and forth. "What a sweet, pretty kitty."

Zoe didn't recognize sarcasm and she smiled happily. "He is a pretty kitty."

Marshmallow Pants started to squirm in her arms. "I think he wants down, Zoe."

She clung tighter, but he was flipping and turning, determined to jump to the floor. Probably to go bribe a bulldog to eat his costume off of him.

"I'll take him," Levi said and reached for the cat.

Zoe lost her grip and the cat leaped onto Levi's chest. He grabbed at it, stumbling off balance and Isabella let out a cry of alarm. I thought the cat was just panicked and would jump to the floor and take off, but before I could blink, the animal was climbing Levi's chest, claws digging in.

"Um . . ." That didn't look good. Did the cat sense Levi was a demon? And should I grab it? I didn't want to get scratched myself, and really, Levi was a big boy. He could handle it. It was just a cat using Levi's black cotton shirt like a climbing wall. No biggie. Cats did that and you just pried them off.

Zoe screamed when Marshmallow Pants reached Levi's chin and bit him. Ouch. That had to sting. Levi was stumbling backward and he connected with the edge of the coffee table. He tripped and fell and the cat went with him as I stood stupidly and blinked. I have crappy reflexes, what can I say? But all I could think was, *What the* . . . ? Now Isabella was shrieking along with Zoe and I was thinking I really needed to come up with a strategy or actually do something. Levi and the cat were a spilled pile of black and white, Levi on his back, Marshmallow Pants on top of him, hissing and spitting.

Okay, I was slow, but not cruel. Someone had to do something besides scream so I ran forward, figuring I could just shove the cat off. But the sweet, pretty kitty was mauling Levi's face, swiping rapidly with front claws like he was scratching to the bottom of the litter box. Levi was twisting, his eyes closed to protect them, his hands struggling to disconnect the cat's claws from his shirt. I pulled and pried, Levi pushed, and together we finally managed to get the cat off of him and onto the carpet. Though the minute the cat was off, he tried to jump right back on Levi.

"Hey!" I yelled, hoping to scare the crazy ball of fur as I shoved him away from Levi again.

Levi sat up, breathing hard, though he looked more mad than scared or hurt. He glared at the cat. "Don't start with me, *Marshmallow Pants*."

The name was spoken with total mockery, and I swear the cat knew he was being dissed because he let out some freaky low growl and tried to take another swipe at Levi. But by then Adam had come over and he picked the cat up with one hand, holding it far away from his own chest as he turned to Zoe. "Does he have a crate?"

"No."

"Well, then he's going in your room and we're closing the door." Adam carried the cat toward the stairs, and I had to admire his take-charge attitude. It must have been the gladiator costume inspiring him.

I looked at Levi, who was still sitting on the floor. "Are you okay?" He had bloody scratches all over his face and neck. Yikes. Those had to sting.

"I'm fine." Levi hauled himself off the floor, scowling.

I bit my fingernail, feeling bad and wondering if I should get him a cold washcloth or something. It wasn't exactly like he could Neosporin his face or slap Band-Aids on or anything, but it seemed like he should at least wash those scratches.

Dirk was staring wide-eyed at Levi, his wrapping paper costume making a wrinkling sound as he moved. "Dude, that was freaky."

"No big deal." Levi turned to Zoe, who was crying big wet tears. "Hey, it's okay, squirt. I'm fine." He ditched the glare he'd been wearing and picked her up and wiped the tears off her cheeks with the bottom of his sleeve.

God. He could be so cute when he was being sweet. I felt a funny little catch in my gut, like indigestion.

"I'm sorry Marshmallow Pants doesn't like you," Zoe said, her words forced out between sobs.

"It's cool. He just knows the score. He wants to be your favorite, but he knows I already am." Levi bounced her a little on his hip and gave her a grin. "Right?"

She nodded, sniffling up a mass of mucus. "Uh-huh."

"So we'll just have to fight it out and see who wins. But you're worth the pain."

"That's true," she said, ever modest, my little sister.

Levi laughed. "Alright, time for you to hit the streets and beg for candy. I'm going to wash my face."

"I'll help you," Isabella offered.

Oh, that was subtle.

Levi raised an eyebrow as he set Zoe down. "I've got it, thanks."

But Isabella followed him upstairs anyway, and five pairs of female eyes followed her movement. The guys were oblivious as usual, but Darla, Madison, Jamie, Sara, and Cecily had all made mental notes. They were so going to go home and call Amber. Her cell phone would be exceeding her minutes that night as they all warned her that Isabella was trying to move in on her man.

Drama-rama. So not my thing.

Though I have to say it seemed to follow me everywhere.

"Let's play a game," Darla suggested.

"What is this, 1962, Barbie?" Dirk asked her, rolling his eyes.

"Well, playing games is better than sitting around staring at each other. Frankly, I can only look at you for so long, Dirk."

He made a face. "I'm going to pick through Kenzie's DVD collection. We should watch a scary movie."

The doorbell rang, and Reggie went to answer it and throw some candy from the dish by the door at my neighbors' kids. My mom and Zoe were heading out the garage door to trick-or-treat themselves and Mom called to me, "Have fun. Be good!"

What does that mean, really? Be good? How does a person know she's falling within her mother's interpretation of Be Good? "Always!" I called back. What else was I going to say? Though I was tempted to just once say, "I will never be good—I am Satan, I want to drink your blood, have orgies, and hurt bunnies." It would totally amuse me, but somehow I don't think my mother would see the humor in it.

"Let the guys watch movies," Madison said. "I'd rather play Bloody Mary Worth. Remember when we used to do that when we were like ten years old at slumber parties." Her eyes rolled back in her head. "I believe in Mary Worth . . ." she droned.

"Let's do it!" Darla said.

The other girls giggled and nodded. Isabella was still missing, probably busy asking Levi for a magic carpet ride in her naked Jasmine outfit.

I shrugged. "Sure." A cranky old dead lady popping up in a mirror was nothing compared to Levi and an open air portal in which random demon prison guards could leap out at me at any given moment.

Bring it on.

Chapter Six

Seven of us stuffed ourselves into my upstairs bath-room for a little conjuring. The guys stayed downstairs to watch a movie, pass out candy, and engorge themselves on pizza, though Reggie did try to slip into the bathroom with us. He'd taken off his dish costume and was just in jeans and a T-shirt, but he didn't exactly blend and Madison immediately kicked him out.

Isabella had joined us, but she was stony-faced and ignoring the questioning looks I kept shooting her.

"What do we do?" Cecily whispered.

"We need a mirror," Madison said, her voice dramatic and low, her hands gesturing for emphasis. "A handheld one. We each have to turn around, look into the mirror in our hand at the reflection from the mirror behind us. We call to Mary, and then she should appear in the mirror, along with the face of our future husband. If she appears alone, as a skull, then it means you'll die before you ever get married."

"Eew," Sara said. "That's gruesome."

My thoughts exactly.

"I'll go first," Darla said.

"There's a compact mirror in the drawer on the left," I told her.

She fished it out. Cecily, who was crammed up against the closed door, flicked off the light at Madison's instructions.

It took a second for my eyes to adjust to the darkness, but I could see the faint outline of Isabella's shoulder next to me, and the top of Darla's teased faux Barbie wig. We were all wedged in with zero space. "Good thing Dirk's not in here with us," I whispered. "Mary Worth would pass out from cologne inhalation."

Everyone laughed.

"I can't see anything," Cecily whispered. "How are you supposed to see in the mirror?"

"I don't know."

But I could see Darla now that my eyes had adjusted, and she held up the compact mirror. "I believe in Mary Worth," she said in a convincing voice. "I believe in Mary Worth. I believe in Mary Worth."

She kept her gaze on the mirror in her hand, but she muttered out of the corner of her mouth to Madison, "Three times, right?"

"Yes."

"Do you see anything?" Sara asked.

"I see . . . I see . . ." Darla shifted the mirror. "A zit on my chin."

I let out the breath I'd been holding as everyone laughed. Not that I had expected her to see anything, but you never knew, did you?

"That stupid acne gel doesn't work," she complained. "This thing is big enough to have its own zip code. Yuck."

She handed the mirror to Sara in disgust.

Sara repeated the process, though she rushed through the words and shifted the mirror around a lot. "All I see is the back of my head."

Isabella took the mirror from Sara when she turned and handed it to her, but Iz was full of attitude about it, I could tell. She was making sounds of impatience and she only used one hand to hold up the mirror. Her voice was bored as she said, "Mary Worth, Mary Worth, Mary Worth."

There was a long pause where Isabella stared into the mirror, longer than I would have expected given her clearly bad mood. But then I saw her eyes widen, and she brought the mirror forward, closer to her. Isabella went still, and all we could hear was each other's suddenly anxious breathing. She was seeing something and we all knew it and we were all too freaked out to ask.

"Iz?" I whispered. "You okay? Do you see something?"

She snapped out of it and actually clicked the compact mirror shut. "No." She scoffed. "Of course not. This whole thing is ridiculous. I'm going back downstairs."

There was jostling as she made her way to the door and opened it, flooding the room with the light from the hallway.

We all blinked at each other.

"Well, that was weird," Darla said. "What's her problem? You're next, Kenzie."

Yeah, because I was just so eager to glance in the mirror and see something crazy. With my luck, Mary Worth would be all old and ugly and holding a pentagram. "Okay." I took the mirror as Cecily closed the door again. I couldn't exactly cop out at my own party.

I fought the urge to close my eyes as I did my three-time chant. Then I looked in the mirror quickly, to get it over with, like pulling off the hot wax strip. If you hesitate, it just makes it worse. There was nothing in the mirror, thank God and then some.

"Nothing for me either," I reported, relief in my voice.

After everyone had a turn and no one saw squat, Cecily turned the light back on and said, "There's another way to figure out who you're going to marry."

"Is this one of the freaky old wives' tales where you have to like pee on wax or something?" Darla asked. "Because I'm not doing that."

Cecily, her bee antennas bouncing as she shook her head, said, "Eew. No, no peeing, I swear. And by the way, I think that's if you're pregnant and want to see if you're having a boy or a girl. You pee into ammonia or something weird like that."

"Oh. Good. So what is this way?"

"You peel an apple, trying to get the whole peel off in one strip, and then you toss it over your shoulder. It will land in the shape of the initial of the guy you're going to marry."

"We'll all be marrying someone named Owen then," Sara said. "Come on, an apple peel is only going to make an O shape."

"Let's try it!" Darla was clearly up for anything.

And I was easy. Why not? I was sure an apple peel couldn't twist itself into an *A*, but then again, it was really hard to visualize marrying Adam anyway. Hello. Sixteen years old. Not looking for the ring quite yet. Just wanted a boyfriend to send me cute texts and to hang out with.

Fortunately, we had a big bag of apples my mom had just picked up at the farmers' market down the road. She loved that we lived in a suburb that still had a few remaining farms and she could score fresh fruit and veggies, and she was going to be confused, but pleased, that we had apparently eaten six apples at our party that wasn't a party.

I left them digging in the kitchen drawers for paring knives, the destroyed (but being repaired) wall covered by a sheet of plastic, as I went to search for Isabella. She wasn't in the family room with the guys, and she wasn't by the front door passing out candy either. I finally found her sitting on my bed in the dark.

"Iz? You okay? What's going on?"

My nightlight was glowing and I could see there were tears on her cheeks. She swiped at them. "Okay. Levi totally blew me off. It was *so* embarrassing. But it's cool. I mean, I suddenly realized that he is totally not my type. And when have I ever been so desperate for a guy to like me that I've thrown myself at him in a Disney princess costume? No one is worth that."

"No, they're not. You don't have to be desperate, you know that. The right guy will be there when he's supposed to, and he'll think you're the bomb." I sat next to her and nudged her shoulder. "Like I do. You're awesome, Iz, and you shouldn't settle for anything less than a guy who is totally into you."

"Yeah, that's what I'm thinking." She finished wiping her face and said, "Ugh. I need a tissue, then I'm going downstairs and having fun. Why waste a good party, right?"

"Exactly. Hey, what did you see in that mirror?" I knew she'd seen something.

She made a sound of impatience. "Oh my God. It was crazy. I actually did see a guy in that mirror, Kenzie. But he was like the biggest nerd ever. Glasses and everything. I've never seen him before, but it had to be like some kind of power of suggestion thing. Like dreaming. Your brain just creates weird random images."

Um. How exactly could your subconscious put a dude's face into a compact mirror in the bathroom when you were wide-awake? I felt a chill crawl up my back and I rubbed my arms.

But Isabella just waved her hand in dismissal. "No big deal. What did you see?"

"Nothing. Nothing at all."

"Oh," she said, and we just stared at each other for a second.

Then she said, "Don't let me marry a nerd," and we both laughed.

"I won't, swear. I've got your back."

"He likes you, you know," she added.

"Who? The nerd in the mirror?" I was confused, as usual.

"No. Levi. He doesn't like me that way, but he does like you as way more than a friend. It was obvious when he was talking about you to me."

I scoffed, even as my heart rate sped up. I was glad the room was still kind of dark, because I could feel a flush marching across my cheeks. "No, he doesn't."

"Well, he does, but it's cool. I understand you didn't do anything to encourage him, and God knows we can't control who we're crushing on. Just be honest with him if he puts it out there, okay? Don't lead him on because you don't want to hurt his feelings. He's got it bad for you, and you'll make it worse if you aren't straight up."

"Okay." Because letting him kiss me was so totally the way to keep things uncomplicated. I almost groaned out loud. "Now let's go try peeling apples and see if the nerd with the glasses has a first initial."

When we got to the kitchen, all our friends were bent over staring at the floor.

"Whose is it?" I asked, trying to check out the apple peel on the floor.

"It's mine," Cecily said. "But I sort of had some problems. I can't peel apples and I just end up with all these little pieces that I've hacked off, so I just threw all of them. What does it look like to you?"

A pile of apple peels. "Um . . . it kind of looks like a *W* to me."

"Ohmigod, it does!" Madison said.

Kind of. If you squinted and tilted your head to the left.

"Maybe it's Wyatt Price," Darla said.

"No!"

Cecily looked horrified and rightly so. Wyatt's width exceeded his height and he had a habit of throwing things at people in outbursts of anger. A cool name like Wyatt was truly wasted on him.

"It's just a game," I told her. "No one is saying Wyatt Price is truly your destiny. Besides, don't we all really make our own destiny?"

She sighed in relief. "That's true. Why don't you do it next, Madison?"

Madison tossed her peel over her left shoulder. It landed in a D shape. "Well, an *R* for Reggie was going to be impossible to get, so I choose to not believe this tradition. Your turn, Kenzie."

"Okay." I peeled an apple from the bag into a nice long red skin strand and set the uneaten apple part down. I turned with my back to the wall and decided I really needed to smack it against the wall and have it crumple into a pile so that it didn't manage to land in an L shape, which was highly likely given the shape of an apple peel. But of course no one else would choose to see it as statistically probable and would say Levi and I were supposed to be together or something insane like that. That was all I needed to complete my night.

I tossed it as hard as I could, expecting to hear a whack as it hit the wall, but I didn't. Turning around I asked, "Where did it go?"

They were all laughing. Isabella grinned at me. "Your aim

sucks. It shot two feet to the left and went straight through the hole between the two pieces of plastic. That was classic."

"It went through the *hole*?" The hole I had made with the minivan? The hole that was supposed to be covered in plastic and that was probably a demon portal? Oopsie. That was probably a bad thing. "I'd better go get it." With my luck my mother would slip on it and break her arm in the garage.

I opened the door to the garage and flicked on the light. I didn't see the peel immediately so I eyed the hole in the drywall suspiciously and inched toward it. I didn't want to be sucked into the portal. I spotted the peel lying next to the tire of the minivan, right under the hole. I went to grab it and let out a yelp, jumping back a foot.

Holy Red Delicious . . . The apple peel was bleeding all over the concrete. A thick, mucky red slime was oozing out like Jell-O blood and there was a hissing sound, like air being let out of a tire.

"Uh . . . don't panic, Kenzie. Just step away from the apple peel." I backed up slowly, keeping my eye on that thing.

I had barely gone two inches in retreat when it growled at me. A freaking apple peel was growling at me like a dog with a juicy bone. I started shuffling backward faster, trying to convince my-self that I did *not* see a pair of angry, glowing black eyes in the sloppy slimy mess the peel had become. When I thought I was close enough to the door, I turned and ran like the total wimp that I was, slamming the kitchen door behind me and locking it.

Of course, there was still a gaping *hole* in the wall, but it was reflex (or pants-wetting fear) that made me turn the deadbolt.

"Where's the apple peel?" Madison asked.

"Couldn't find it," I said breathlessly, trying to calm my pounding heart. "I need to tell Levi something. Be right back." I booked it into the family room, knowing my friends were probably questioning my sanity, but not caring. I didn't even want to be in the kitchen, let alone within grabbing distance of that peel/portal. I shuddered as I visualized that disgusting mess again.

Yeah, demon slayer. So me. Not. I was afraid of fruit, which was just totally pathetic.

The guys were watching *Halloween* on DVD and three of the seven of them glanced at me as I came into the room and hovered. Dirk stuck his tongue out at me, Adam gave me a look of longing like he wished it was me on the couch next to him instead of Reggie (me too, would give anything to be encircled in Adam's arm watching scary events unfold instead of living them), and Levi looked over at me, mildly curious.

Dilemma. How did I let Levi know I wanted to talk to him without making Adam mad? I continued to hover behind the couch waiting for them to stop caring what I was doing and turn back around, hopefully in the order I wanted: Dirk, Adam, Levi. When I didn't respond to Dirk's "pay attention to me" tongue-out-of-mouth gesture, he lost interest and went back to watching Michael Myers slice people. One down. Both Adam and Levi were still looking at me. I looked back.

We were all just looking.

Not going to get anywhere that way, but how could I let Levi know we had a problem without Adam's jumping on the jealousy train?

"What's up?" Adam said. "You going to watch the movie with us?"

"Actually, I'm going to check on the cat. We probably should have taken that angel costume off of him before we locked him up." True, but had I cared until I needed an excuse to leave the room? Not really, which probably made me an evil person, for which I was going to feel bad about later, after I discussed bleeding face–filled apple peel with Levi.

"Okay. Then come sit with me," Adam said.

"Of course," I said with a forced smile. Perfect girlfriend, that was me. (Insert anxious emoticon here.)

I ran up the stairs hoping that Levi would somehow get the hint I never gave and follow me. On the landing, I tripped over a pile of something that shouldn't be lying there and went down.

"Ow, get off me!" my brother Brandon yelled, shoving at my legs.

Peeling myself off his gut, I glared at him. "What are you doing lying on the floor in the dark? I could have broken my ankle!"

"You could break your ankle standing still in bubble wrap." Brandon's cell phone chimed and still sprawled out on his back he flicked it open, obviously reading a text.

Sticking my tongue out seemed like the only recourse for his rudeness, so I did that absentmindedly and left him to his random hallway weirdness.

Opening the door to Zoe's room, I flicked on the light and found Marshmallow Pants crashed out on Zoe's zebra-striped chaise, looking fluffy and annoyed, even in his sleep, his angel halo crooked. Maybe it was just the type of cat, but I swear every time I looked at him MP was wearing his angry eyes. It was possible he was still recovering from whatever tragedy had landed him in our driveway or maybe he was just a crank.

Carefully I slid the strap out from under his furry chin (do cats even have chins?) and lifted the halo off and tossed it on Zoe's desk. MP opened his eyes, checked me out, licked his paw, then laid his head back down, eyes drifting closed again. Okay, now what? If the cat was sleeping he couldn't be that miserable in his satin outfit, so I'd just leave it for now, but how long did I wait for Levi to show up when he didn't know he was supposed to show up? Everyone was going to start to wonder where I was.

Panic had me pacing in my Mary Janes, my sweaty hands rubbing over the front of my blue trapeze dress.

I tried to tell myself it was no big deal. It was just an apple peel. Whatever. No one had tried to kill me, snatch me, molest me.

Just a piece of fruit skin.

With a face. Bloody slime. And the ability to growl.

The door to Zoe's room opened and I whirled, imagining a giant raging apple rolling in to crush me with its fiber content.

It was Levi. Almost the same thing.

"What are you doing?" he asked. "You look like you could cry at any given second."

Hello. I don't think so. "I'm not going to cry. I'm just trying to have this party and want everyone to have a good time and not know that my house is possessed."

"The house is not possessed. What has you so overdramatic?" Levi strolled in and shut the door behind him. "Oh, wait. You're always overdramatic."

"Ha ha, aren't we funny. Never. Okay, so I threw my apple peel over my shoulder—"

He interrupted me. "Why would you do that?"

"It's not important! But I threw it too hard and it went through the gap in the plastic in the hole in the kitchen wall and into the garage." I paused for air. "Then I went to get it and it was by the van and it was oozing."

"Oozing?" His eyebrow went up.

"Like the way my shower drain did last time. Oozing this foul nasty red slime like open heart surgery and, and, I don't know . . . it was just seriously yucky."

"Yucky?"

"Yes, yucky!" Why was he repeating everything I said? "Then it had a face in it."

"In the apple peel?"

"Yes. And it growled at me. So what was it and what do we do?"

I felt worried. I sounded worried. I was sure I looked worried. Levi? Not so much. He might as well have been chillin' with a Dr Pepper and a doughnut in front of Cartoon Network.

"Well, it's obvious that when the peel went through the portal, a prison guard used it as a medium. But it's still stuck in the apple peel, so it's no big deal. And *we* don't do anything. *You* have to close the portal."

"Oh, here we go. Kenzie do this, do that, but I'm sorry, I can't tell you what to do, how to do it, and even where to do it. Just wander around knowing nothing and trying to close whatever it might be wherever it might be." I was pacing again and gesturing and biting my fingernails. "It's not like closing a dresser drawer here!" I paused and looked at him. "Is it?"

He shook his head.

Blech. Of course not. I started ranting again. "I need something to work with here! I can't be wandering around in Moron Land stumbling over random demon prison guards. If I'm going to be a slayer—which I don't want to be, but it seems like I have zippo for choices—then I need some knowledge, some skills."

Levi was smiling. Grinning actually, and it ticked me off. "What?" I asked, as grouchy with him as Marshmallow Pants had been in the family room. Too bad I didn't have any handy razor-sharp claws. I could add my artwork to his face alongside the cat's stinging red scratches.

"You're handling this all really well."

"Don't mock me!" I glanced around for something to whip at him, infuriated.

"I'm not!" He actually looked shocked and he walked over to me. "I'm seriously not. I meant it. I know none of this has been easy and you've been cool with it all along. I know I popped out of your drain and screwed up your life and you're dealing really well. I . . . ."

"What?" I asked, still feeling put out but also feeling like if he kept throwing compliments my way I could get over it.

"I really respect you. Like you. A lot."

Okay. You see what's coming here, don't you?

I melted a little. Let him take my hand and look at me pleadingly with those pale green eyes.

"K, I would help you if I could. I feel really bad about everything and I think of you as like my best friend, and I don't want this to be hard for you."

He thought of me as his best friend? That was really sweet.

"Levi . . . it's fine. I know you're not doing it on purpose. But the Underworld's rules suck, you know. I'm just saying."

"They do. But I'll try to help you. I really will."

And then he kissed me.

Yep. He did it again.

And do you think I learned *anything* from the first time?

No. Nothing. Nada.

Zip. Zero.

My first thought was *No way*. I couldn't believe he was just leaning in and going for it all over again after apologizing for doing it the first time. My second thought, post–lip connection, was *Wow*. The demon could kiss.

It was like when you take the first big bite of pink cotton candy and it melts in your mouth in a massive sugar puddle and your brain sort of freezes and your body jolts and your mouth zings, and after a few seconds you're with it enough to think, *Good Stuff*.

The kiss was Good Stuff.

Proving that I was in fact a horrible person, I didn't even hesitate once I realized the kiss was awesome, but slid my hands around his neck and kissed him back, our bodies pressing together. I could hear his breathing getting faster, feel the warmth of his chest against mine, and the tightening of his fingers on my waist. No idea where we thought we were going with it, but we were just going.

I had no clue how much time had passed, but it was likely a new president had taken office and we had completely missed our high school graduation while we were busy making out, and I didn't really care.

Until the door to Zoe's room opened and somewhere in the back of my foggy brain I realized that was a bad thing.

We were caught.

Oh. My. God.

I jerked back away from Levi and turned to see who it was, wiping my wet lips, rubbing my damp hands on my dress, trying to calm my heart down, and praying like crazy that it was just my sister or even my mother. That wouldn't be nearly as bad as anyone else at the party.

But it wasn't just anyone.

It was Adam.

$#@!%!

Now that was bad. Mucho Bad. Grande Bad. I couldn't think, couldn't speak, could only stare at him, registering the hurt and horror on his very, very cute face.

Adam didn't say anything.

Levi was quiet too, for once.

There was a long awful pause where I felt all the tortilla chips I'd eaten churn and start to crawl back up my throat.

Then Adam just turned and left, slamming the door shut behind him.

I could hear his feet on the steps as he ran down them.

"I'm sorry, Kenzie," Levi said into the stunned silence, and I felt my whole head go hot, then clammy. "I didn't mean to do that."

Chapter Seven

I sucked.

Plain and simple.

There I was, dating the guy I had crushed on for a year, who treated me like a rock star, and who put up with my being grounded for driving a minivan through my kitchen, whose friends were nice to me, and who had defended me against his mother, and what did I do?

Made out with a demon.

Who did that????

Me. Kenzie Sutcliffe. Stupidest sixteen-year-old on planet Earth. That's who.

I stood there gasping for air, feeling sick to my gut, no clue what to do to make it all better. To make it go away.

"I'll talk to Adam," Levi said.

That set me into motion. "No!" I said, running for the door. "That will only make it worse. I mean, what can you possibly say?"

"That it was all my fault," he said, following me.

I moved faster, out of my room and down the hall, wanting away from Levi, my very own walking talking Mistake. I had no clue what I could possibly say to Adam, but I had to say something. Apologize. Beg for forgiveness. The usual things you do when its clear a relationship has landed at the bottom of the toilet and its all your fault.

But when I hit the family room and glanced wildly around, Dirk said, "What's going on? Adam tore out of here."

"He left?"

"Yep. A minute ago. Looking like he'd taken a baseball bat in the face."

Ouch. Twist the screw of my guilt a little harder. I ran for the front door, ignoring Levi's suggestion to just let him go, and hauling myself as fast as my heels could take me. Adam was backing out of the driveway in his truck, so I waved my arms and called to him. "Adam! Stop. Please."

To my amazement, he actually did. He rolled the window down when I got to the driver's side and just stared at me, his face white in the dark. "What?" he asked.

"It wasn't what it looked like," I said.

Yeah, good one, Kenzie. Because everyone always believes that lame, completely stupid, illogical, I'm-caught-and-don't-want-to-admit-it load of crap I had just handed him.

He clearly agreed because he scoffed. "Really. It looked like you were making out with Levi to me. That's not what it was?" "No . . . it was a kiss. Guess you were right about the fact that he likes me. I honestly had no idea," I said, biting my lip and trying to look innocent, knowing I was lying, knowing he knew I was lying, hating myself and a certain houseguest from hell and the fact that I couldn't do anything without screwing it up.

"You were kissing him back," he pointed out.

"I don't think . . ." I couldn't do it. It was pointless to lie when he had seen me. "I'm sorry," I said instead. "I didn't mean . . ."

Adam's jaw twitched. "Bye, Kenzie." Then he looked behind him and backed up slowly to avoid the roaming packs of trick-or-treaters, and I was left standing there, the wind cutting through my trapeze dress and my heart honestly actually truly breaking.

I had no idea it could even feel that way—sort of squeezed and crushed and flat and empty. I had fun with Adam. His smile made me smile. He could pick me up and swing me around even though I was five foot nine. He was the only person who said "dude" repeatedly and it didn't annoy me.

Dude, it hurt. I had just ruined the rest of my junior year of high school.

I walked inside, determined to avoid everyone and run up to my room and let the tears that were begging to run down my face a chance to do their thing.

Except everyone was huddled ten feet from the front door, between me and the stairs to privacy. There was whispering, and

Justin was rubbing Darla's back, and there were expressions of shock and I knew then that they knew . . .

Isabella stalked up to me in her Jasmine costume, which at some point had been altered by the addition of an Abercrombie T-shirt that I was pretty sure was Levi's. Iz's mouth was tight, her face pale, her hands on her hips.

"Did you make out with Levi?" she asked me, not even bothering to keep her voice down.

Panicked, I just stared at her. I couldn't answer that with a dozen people watching me in horrified curiosity.

"Hey, Isabella," Levi said, coming to my side. "Leave Kenzie alone. It's not her fault."

Well, that just confirmed it was all true. I closed my eyes for a brief second. Not that anyone doubted it, because clearly Adam had told someone when he'd left, who in turn had told the whole room, and we weren't going to be able to deny it. But Levi could have allowed me that illusion just a little longer.

And how was it not my fault, exactly? I was there, wasn't I? I had kissed Levi because I had wanted it (eek, did I just admit that?). But it was time to take responsibility for it.

"So you did?" Isabella asked, darting her eyes from Levi to me again.

"Yes," I said. "And we both know it shouldn't have happened, and I'm really sorry that I hurt . . . anyone." Meaning both Adam and her. I didn't think she would want her crush on Levi broadcast.

"Uh-oh," Darla said.

"Dude," Dirk said.

"Levi," Justin said. "Man, Adam's your friend. What's up with that?"

After that, it all disintegrated into tears, arguing, hands thrown up in the air, and lots of bodies stalking their way out of my house.

When Isabella left, declaring us no longer best friends, I couldn't deal. I left the stragglers who were still hanging around for Levi to deal with and I ran upstairs and flung myself onto my bed as hard as I possibly could and cried until my eyes were swollen, my nose was running, and my throat was raspy.

Levi knocked on my locked door four times and gave me lots of pleading, "Can we talk about this?" lines, but I totally ignored him.

"I can hear you crying," he said the second time he showed up.

Yeah, no duh. So what? I buried my face in my pillow and contemplated my fate now that everyone in the world hated my guts.

The last time he actually said, "If you don't at least answer me and let me know you're alive, I'm breaking this damn door down."

Though part of me was curious to see if he actually would, I didn't want the consequences from my father if more damage to the house occurred. Neither did I want Levi actually anywhere near me. So I dragged my wet, dripping, drooling head off my pillow and yelled, "Leave me alone!"

"Good, you're okay," he said, in obvious relief.

Okay? *Okay?* I was so not okay.

Monday. Always a less than exciting day. But this was Monday the day after Halloween. The traditional Day of the Dead. And in this case, day of my dead social career.

It was—and I know this totally sounds overdramatic, but really, if you had been there, you would agree—the single worst day of my entire life.

No one was talking to me. No one. Not even friends I'd had for years, not even random weirdos who normally look for anyone to glom on to. I was like bad breath. Moldy cheese. Acne. Teen pregnancy. Everyone was trying to avoid me. Weren't we too old for this? Hadn't we left all this clique crap behind us back in middle school? Hadn't we learned not to judge until we knew the whole story?

Of course, the whole story was that I had in fact made out with Levi in my baby sister's bedroom at a Halloween party I had thrown for the purpose of getting my best friend together with Levi and to which I had invited primarily my boyfriend's friends, resulting in total humiliation for cheated-on boyfriend and utter devastation for best friend.

Blech. I wouldn't talk to me either.

I spent the day in silence, moving from class to class, feeling like I was going to throw up as people whispered behind my back, avoided my eyes, and gave lame excuses why they couldn't sit with

me at lunch or couldn't walk with me to English or math or whatever the way they usually did.

"Ohmigod! Like I totally forgot I have to pick up a flyer for
the French trip right now. I'll catch up with you later, Kenzie."

Uh-huh.

Or "Wow, um, I have to go talk to my counselor."

Because anyone ever willingly does that.

Others like Darla said it straight out. "I can't talk to you because Reggie is best friends with Adam."

But the best was Madison's: "I'm allergic to your two-faced-
ness."

Ouch.

Literature came to life and actually made sense to me for the
first time ever. I was freaking Hester Prynne from *The Scarlet Let-
ter*, shunned and ashamed, and it sucked. Royally.

I started imagining the crowds actually parting as I walked
through the halls, determined not to get any of my moral dirt on
them and soil their pristine selves and souls. Hey, I was a theater
junkie, remember? It wasn't a stretch for my imagination to go
there, especially since I was lonely as my day of silence rolled on.
And picturing myself in costume, on a stage, was the only way I
could get through the day.

It was bad enough that I had ruined my relationship with
Adam, but Isabella had been my best friend for five years. We did
everything together. She had been there through puberty and
sleepovers and crushes and bad auditions and I couldn't believe
the cold look she shot me at lunch when I gave her a smile and

tried to talk to her. I knew what I had done was totally wrong, but she had told me Levi wasn't interested in her, so I wasn't exactly sure why she was mad. Okay, not true, I knew why she was mad. There's a girlfriend rule with guys and I had broken it. I should have waited a few months before hooking up with Levi, and that should have been only after I got her consent and permission to pursue. Girl Rule.

So, yeah, I wouldn't like me much either, and I actually darted into the bathroom after lunch to wipe tears from my eyes. I had to figure out a way to get Isabella to talk to me so I could apologize and grovel and make it all right or I was going to curl up into a ball and cease to exist.

But first, I had to go to Anatomy and Physiology class, where I just happened to share a lab desk with Adam Birmingham, my now ex-boyfriend. Good times. Probably as fun as stabbing myself in the eye repeatedly with a fetal pig dissection knife. After it was used in a dissection.

Since I wasn't interested in lingering in the halls, which would only make it even more obvious how totally ignored I was, I was already sitting in class when Adam came in. He dropped his books down on the desk so hard, I actually jumped. Not looking at me, he sat down and moved his chair as far away from me as possible.

"Adam," I said. "We need to talk."

He didn't even look over at me, and I knew then that he wasn't mad, he was hurt. If he were just angry, he would turn and say something rude, maybe even yell at me. But he wasn't. He couldn't even look at me, and that meant he was hurt, which somehow was absolutely worse. I was feeling about as wanted as a case of *E. coli.*

"No, we don't," he said.

"I need to tell you I'm sorry," I said in an urgent whisper, aware that classmates were shooting curious glances our way.

"Whatever."

Now you would think that I would have just quit there. That given we were in public and it was absolutely clear how he felt about me right at the moment, that I would have just slumped over in my chair and dropped the subject.

Not me. I thought "whatever" wasn't exactly the same as telling me to eat a fetal pig and die, so it seemed like maybe if I just went for it, I could get some kind of result I might actually like.

Hey, I never said I was the sharpest crayon in the box. Just the most hopeful.

So that's why I said, "Thanks for forgiving me, I really am completely and utterly sorry. So do you want to come over tonight? We can do homework."

You know that moment in TV shows where the music grinds to a halt and all the actors turn and look straight at the camera? I swear I could actually hear the beat cut out and the sound effect of squealing tires as Adam swiveled to look at me for the first time since he'd walked into the room. His expression was well, not exactly lovey-kissy.

"Are you *serious?*" he asked.

Was that a trick question?

"We're not doing homework together. We're done."

"Done?" I asked, in case I had somehow misinterpreted what that meant, which of course, I knew I hadn't and had known since the second my lips had peeled off of Levi's and turned to see Adam standing there.

"Yes. Done. Have a good time with Levi, Kenzie." Adam turned resolutely back to his textbook and pretended an interest in science for the first time all semester.

Waahh. My lip trembled, my gut churned, and I knew I was pouting, but there was nothing I could do so I flipped open my book and stared at the innards of a chimp as they removed his heart for a transplant. It was disturbing enough that I was momentarily distracted by compassion for the poor little monkey. Yeesh. I thought I had it bad.

And where was Levi during Kenzie's Terrible, Horrible, No-Good, Very Bad Day?

He was with Amber Jansen, his über-perfect girlfriend who had decided that she was going to Stand By Her Man.

Gag.

They were walking around school holding hands and looking like they had torn down their metaphorical townhouse and rebuilt a new one from the ground up. It had taken a tragedy, a mistake, a disastrous almost end to their relationship for them to see the true depth of their devotion to each other.

Can you say nauseating?

Somewhere between slunking down the hall after math class

trying to hold my head up both literally and figuratively, and grabbing my coat out of my locker in relief that the day from hell was finally over, I had a radical thought.

Things were bad. Not that that was the radical thought. But really, they were bad. I had taken seriously ugly to a whole new level since Levi had popped out of the portal into my life.

Yeah, things had been boring before he arrived, but they had been normal. I'd had someone to eat lunch with, a situation I'd never take for granted again. Now it was looking like I might have to transfer schools if I ever wanted to have anyone to talk to ever again, and it was essentially because of Levi.

The demon who told me I was the only one who could close the portal, because I was a demon slayer.

Me, demon slayer. Levi, demon.

Couldn't I send Levi back to hell?

Thereby restoring peace and calm to my existence?

Huh.

Now that was an idea worth exploring.

Chapter Eight

A Pop-Tart was in order after the day I'd had. I suffered through the bus—yes, the bus, since my license didn't exist
and Levi was staying after school for soccer practice—and was really looking forward to the comfort of my own home where
there was sugar and people who didn't hate me.

Except that Mike, the giant construction worker, was in my
kitchen with his co-workers, and there were white plastic pipes
laid out all across the floor blocking the entry to the pantry where
frosted rectangles of processed food waited to comfort me. It
didn't help my frustration to think about the fact that it was my
fault, and well, ultimately Levi's, that the wall had been destroyed
in the first place, thus creating my current lack of privacy.

Oh, yeah. The demon had to go.

I liked Levi.

We've established that.

I even liked kissing him.

I could admit it in the privacy of my own head.

But our relationship was not good for me, my sanity, or my social life.

So he needed to take his little self and his portals back from whence he came. (Wasn't that the nerdiest expression? *Loved* it and had been waiting to use it.)

The question was how. That was always the question.

I eyed Mike suspiciously. If he was a demon, wouldn't he know how to close the portal? Or how to send Levi back? He didn't look bright, and he didn't exactly look evil either, but I couldn't trust him for obvious reasons. But maybe if I talked to him, I could squeeze some info from him.

Ten minutes later I had figured out that my spy skills sucked. While I knew I was a good actress and could play the role of Teen Seeking Friendship with Mike, I had no clue how to interrogate.

"Hi," I said to him with a smile, easing toward the pantry. Might as well snag my Pop-Tart while I was taking one for Team Slayer.

"Hey," he said, returning my smile with a big cheesy grin. "What's up?"

"Not much. Just hungry." Okay, now what? *So are you from here or hell originally?* was probably a little too obvious. "Um . . . is this your full-time job?"

"Yep. Since I graduated last year." He jerked his thumb over to the two guys in the garage who were doing mysterious things to the exposed plumbing on the damaged wall. "It's a family business. My father and my uncle."

"Wow, I really think I would kill my father if I had to work with him. Actually, he would probably kill me," I said, focus on my goal already shot as I pictured eight-hour days with my dad, Bill "Do It My Way" Sutcliffe.

Mike laughed, which earned him a sharp look from one of the two men.

"You workin' or flirtin'?" either his dad or uncle asked. It wasn't the one who'd made the creepy brother comment when I had hugged Levi in the kitchen on Saturday.

Making a face, Mike squatted down and went back to measuring and marking lines on the white plastic tubie things.

"Sorry," he murmured, glancing up at me ruefully. "That's my dad."

I hopped up onto the island so I wouldn't be in his way and unwrapped my Pop-Tart. "How do you know what you're doing?" I asked, curious. It all just looked like a bunch of random pipes running through our wall. How did these guys actually know what was what and where it went?

"Experience. They've been dragging me on jobs since I was eight."

"Really? How old are you now?" Was I flirting? I bit my food and mentally smacked myself. Just because it was looking less and less likely that he was a demon given that his father and uncle were with him, that didn't mean I should flirt. He really was not my type, as noted earlier.

"Just turned nineteen last week."

"Oh, happy birthday." See, too old for me. I was totally relieved. Actually, what I was was desperate for someone to talk to. It had been a long, lonely day.

"Thanks. How old are you?"

"Sixteen," I said through a mouthful, swinging my legs as I checked out his butt. Hey, I could look, right? It was right there, bent over the pipes, in a pair of worn jeans. "I'm a junior at West Shore."

"Really?" He sounded surprised. "You look older than that."

"Yeah, most people mistake me for thirty-five."

Mike laughed and set down his measuring tape. "So is the dude who lives here your boyfriend?"

"Levi? No. I don't have a boyfriend." Whimper. "He's a friend of the family." Is that what we were calling him? "And he's living here while his parents get divorced and hurl plates at each other."

"Oh, that sucks for him."

More like it sucked for me. "Yeah."

"So you want to go out sometime? Like maybe Friday night?"

I had a feeling he was going to get there eventually, but Mike didn't waste any time. I paused, thinking of all the people my dating Mike would set off. Parents, Levi, Adam, Isabella, Amber Jansen—the list was as long as my arm. Figuring I was in enough trouble, and given that Mike didn't really do it for me anyway, I shook my head. "I can't. I'm grounded. I did this, you know." I gestured to the wall his family business was responsible for fixing.

His eyebrows shot up as he looked at me from the floor. "How did you do that?"

"Drove the minivan through the wall," I said, taking another bite of Pop-Tart. "Bad scene, trust me."

He laughed. "Guess so. Don't think I'll be getting in a car with you behind the wheel."

"No one will. I can't drive until I'm eighteen." Ugh. It sounded even worse out loud.

"Mike! Get over here," his dad yelled from the garage.

Rolling his eyes at me, Mike slowly rose to his feet. "Guess I'll catch you later, Kenzie," he said with a smile.

"Sure." I sat there for a minute and thought about how I closed the water portal by taking out the plumbing in the wall with the van. This was an air portal, right? How did you kill an air source? Taking away air wasn't exactly an easy thing to do. Did you suck it? Vacuum it?

I sat up straighter. Vacuum. That might work.

Which is how I found myself industriously vacuuming up the sawdust from the construction that night after dinner. Without explaining what I was doing, I had just gone to the closet, pulled out the vacuum, and cleaned up the mess on the floor. I then dragged it into the garage, sucked every speck of dust up, and undid the hose. Staring at the spot where the apple peel had been, I wondered what had happened to it. Maybe Levi had cleaned it up or maybe it had just evaporated. There was no telling.

My mother stuck her head out the garage door. "Wow, thanks, Kenzie. I appreciate you cleaning up. All that dust is hard to deal with."

"Sure, Mom." Good daughter, that was me. Cleaning the house and closing demon portals.

I was taking the hose and just sucking at the air in and around the hole when Levi appeared in the doorway. "What are you doing?" he asked.

"Vacuuming."

"The air?"

"Yes. Go away." He wasn't going to tell me anything, I wasn't going to tell him anything.

He just stood there. "We need to talk."

I glanced at his cat-scratched face. "No, we don't." The vacuum sucked in some of the plastic and I winced as I ripped it back out. I had nothing to say to Levi.

The cat streaked past Levi's legs.

"Marshmallow Pants!" Zoe screamed, darting around Levi too in pursuit of her new pet.

I turned off the vacuum. "Is that cat wearing a dress?"

Levi started laughing. "Yes. Pink with flowers. That's hilarious."

Shaking my head, I watched the cat run under the van and stare at us with black eyes. I wasn't a cat person. They always seemed like they were secretly plotting the destruction of the human race. And despite the cutesy name Zoe had given it, this one struck me as slightly evil.

"Levi, you have to get him for me!" Zoe pleaded.

I didn't see what the big deal was. The garage door to the driveway was closed, so it wasn't like the cat could go anywhere. But the tears of a cute five-year-old blonde always resulted in action. Before I could say Marshmallow Pants, Levi was crawling on the ground attempting to coax the cat forward so he could grab her. Him. Whatever it was. I wasn't sure we had even bothered to officially determine the cat's gender. I think my mother was secretly hoping the cat would run away before she had to go so far as to take him to the vet and get him a license.

"Come here, kitty, kitty," Levi said.

The cat hissed.

Levi reached for it and got a swat on the hand.

"Come on, I'm serious."

The cat made a coughing sound, then threw up right in front of Levi.

Levi turned his head and wrinkled his nose. "Sick, Otis."

"Who's Otis?" Zoe asked, leaning over Levi to check out the vomit.

"It's my nickname for the cat. He looks like an Otis to me."

"Well, he won't come to you unless you call him by his real name, Marshmallow Pants," Zoe said with authority.

"Right. Marshmallow Pants, this ground is cold and your puke smells. So come out. Now." Levi grabbed the cat and dragged and wrestled and pulled him out from under the van.

I was clipping the vacuum attachment back on and watching in amusement when we all heard my mother scream from the house. It sounded like something had ripped its face off in front of her, there was so much fear in her voice.

Abandoning the vacuum, I ran, as did Levi, who was still struggling to hold the cat, and Zoe.

Inside the kitchen my mother was white-faced and pointing to the floor. "Levi," she said in a shaky voice, "I hope you weren't attached to your gym shoes."

"What?"

We all followed her finger and I reared back. "Oh, nasty!" There was a dead mouse—actually, just a mouse head—bloody and gruesome, sticking up out of Levi's shoe.

"I think Marshmallow Pants left you a present," my mom added, swallowing hard. "Oh, that's so gross."

Zoe screamed.

The cat jumped down out of Levi's grip and ran, though he paused at the edge of the family room and gave one glance back at us before tearing off for parts unknown.

"We have *mice*?" I asked, horrified.

"Not if I have anything to say about it," my mom announced. "I'm calling the exterminator in the morning." Then she yelled, "Bill! I need you in the kitchen. Bill!"

"I can get it, Mrs. S." Levi grimaced, but he picked up his shoe and headed for the garage, presumably to dump the head in the trash can.

When he got back, he actually went and put his gym shoe in the washing machine.

"You're keeping that?" Eew. Double eew. Triple eew.

"There's just a little blood and fur on it. It will wash right off. These shoes cost ninety bucks."

A budget-conscious demon. He was taking the whole thing really well, given that his face looked like he'd lost a battle with a pricker bush and he'd had his shoe turned into a burial ground for a rodent.

It wasn't until after ten that night when I caught Levi trying to throw Marshmallow Pants out onto the back deck that I realized he might be more annoyed than he was letting on.

"What are you doing?" I asked him, even though it was obvious.

He jumped, clearly clueless that anyone was around. "Um, nothing."

"You just stuck that cat outside. It's November. It's forty degrees out there."

"So? He has a lot of fur. And I think he's actually an outdoor cat," Levi said, crossing his arms over his chest and shutting the sliding door to the deck closed on Marshmallow Pants. "I think he wants to run around and kill mice outside."

"He's standing on the deck by the door, staring into the house and meowing," I pointed out. The cat looked like he had been betrayed. He was just sitting there, his mewling faint but obvious.

So the Nice Guy Demon didn't like cats any more than I did. I went over and opened the door, watching the cat dart back in.

"What did you do that for?" Levi asked, annoyed.

I wasn't sure, but it seemed mean to leave it out there when it wanted in. "Because I'm saving Zoe's hero worship of you. She would be destroyed if she knew you tortured her cat."

"I wasn't torturing it! I just sent it outside to hunt at will. Where it can drop dead mice in the grass, instead of my shoe."

"Well, it's back in the house now. Sorry." Not really. Despite the gross factor, it was kind of funny that the cat had chosen Levi's shoe to make his deposit in.

"I need to talk to you," he said, hiking his jeans back up on his hips.

"Nope, no, you don't," I said cheerfully, determined not to think about how it had felt to have him kiss me. And there was going to be no talking about it. Ever.

"But it's important."

"So talk to Amber about it. You know, since you have a girl-friend." Okay, bitterness was squeaking out. Time to leave the room.

"K-Slay, come on . . ."

Argh. I hated it when he called me that stupid demon slayer nickname he'd given me. "I can't believe this is my life!" I exploded. "No one will talk to me, NO ONE, except for you. What kind of a cruel irony is that?"

"Okay, drama queen, now that that's out of your system, can we be rational for a minute?"

No. No, we couldn't. I stuck my tongue out at him and stomped off to my room to write an e-mail to Isabella begging her to forgive me before I was actually forced out of desperation to talk to Levi.

Chapter Nine

After fourteen days that felt like four hundred as a complete social pariah, I decided I was willing to talk to Levi. My thought when the Incident first went down was that if Levi and I talked at school, people would really think we were actually a couple, which (a) wasn't true, (b) would label me a boyfriend stealer, and (c) eew. Then when it became obvious in about a minute that Levi and Amber were still West Shore's Cutest Couple (aside from those cat scratches on Levi's mug), I figured it would really look weird if I talked to him at school. Like I was still dangling after him in a state of desperation, and maybe I was down and out but I had my pride.

But two weeks later I was willing to talk to anyone that could form sentences and didn't look at me like I was toxic waste. I was talking to the baggers at the grocery store, which I offered to voluntarily go to with my mother, and I was playing Polly Pockets with Zoe just to hear the sound of my own voice. If it wasn't for play practice at the theater two nights a week, I would have probably literally gone insane.

I kind of thought everyone would thaw out. I mean, it wasn't like I'd started dating a teacher or had become an overnight Internet porn sensation. But no, there was no thawing. I was still getting the tundra treatment and my e-mails and voice mails to Isabella were going unanswered, which initially upset me, then hurt me, then ticked me off. Five years of friendship and she wasn't even going to let me apologize? I would have listened to her, and that stung.

My nightly sawdust vacuuming did nothing but keep the kitchen clean and score me some brownie points with my mom, and as far as I knew, the portal was still wide open. I figured it was time to suck it up (my pride, not the portal) and actually talk to Levi if I ever wanted to squeeze any info about closing it out of him.

And I was still contemplating sending him back. How to Lose Levi in Ten Days was starting to hold some serious appeal.

I made a list of pros and cons:

Pros

- Never again would I have to hear that stupid nickname, K-Slay.

- Amber Jansen would be boyfriendless, with no idea why he had dumped her, since he would just disappear like a thief in the night (though knowing her, she'd move in on new prey within two days).

• I wouldn't have to be chauffeured around by Levi anymore and listen to his cracks on my bad driving.

• No evil entities would try to enter my house to retrieve him.

• I wouldn't have to suffer his popularity while I rotted in Loserville.

• No more watching everyone fall for his sweetness and light act.

• My life would be normal again.

Cons

• I would miss him.

Disgusted at myself, I ripped the list up and tossed it in the trash. Why exactly would I miss him? No clue.

Further confirmed when I had to sit next to him in the minivan on the way to the zoo to help my mother chaperone Zoe's latest Girl Scout outing.

I was just sitting there, biting my fingernails as I stared out the window when my finger was suddenly jerked out of my mouth. I turned to glare at Levi. "What?"

"Quit biting your fingernails. It's gross. You're ripping pieces of them off and spitting them out. I'm going to toss my Frosted Flakes."

Feeling like I might suddenly cry, I said, "I don't like you," and studied my nails so he could see how on the edge I was. Yuck. Maybe Levi had a point. My nails looked like I'd taken the tips to a cheese grater, my midnight blue polish shredded.

"Yeah, because you haven't said *that* yet today. I was getting worried we might go a full day without you declaring your dislike."

"Biting nails is gross," Zoe piped up, craning her neck to see us in the backseat.

Anyone who still needs a booster seat should not be entitled to an opinion. On anything. "No one asked you, diva."

Zoe shot me a look of rebuke. "Mom! Kenzie called me diva."

"Kenzie, stop calling your sister names!" My mom sounded huffy and annoyed as we pulled into the elementary school parking lot to collect the other girls who would be riding with us.

I huddled against the window and felt sorry for myself. I was good at it.

Levi nudged me with his knee. I glanced over at him and he gave me a dorky smile full of teeth, his eyebrows going up and down. "Come on. We'll have fun at the zoo. In the aquatics building we can watch the piranhas bite the heads off minnows and you can pretend they're me."

"Why pretend they're you?" I said. "Let's just toss you into the tank and see what happens."

He pinched my cheeks like he was my aunt Mary. "You're so cute when you're bitter."

I was about to smack him when he tilted his head and listened, like he heard something.

"What?" I knew that look. It was his Demon Danger Alert look.

But he just shook his head, and refocused on me, smiling. "Nothing."

My mom had parked and was undoing her seatbelt. "Okay, I'm going to go talk to the other troop leader and see who we're taking in our car."

"I'm going with you," Zoe said.

I didn't see any point in standing around in the cold November morning while the moms negotiated and the kindergartners ran around in circles on the blacktop, so I stayed in the van and worried. Easy enough.

Especially since Levi was on the floor of the van crawling around on all fours and whispering in . . . was that Latin?

"Uh . . . what are you doing?" I unbuckled my seatbelt and pulled my legs up onto the seat. If a snake or something was on the floor, I didn't want to touch it. No thanks. Pass.

"Otis," Levi snarled.

Otis? What or who was that? And where had I heard that before?

A second later a triumphant looking Levi dragged a hissing Marshmallow Pants out from under the seat. "Hah, got you, you furry little freak."

That earned him a bite on the arm, which had Levi hissing like the cat.

"What is he doing in here?" I asked. "Nice outfit, MP."

The cat was wearing a hot pink onesie. It didn't look conducive to litter-box usage, but I was guessing Zoe hadn't thought that far ahead.

Levi was opening the door and after a second I realized he was just going to drop the cat in the parking lot. "What are you doing? You can't throw that cat out!" I grabbed his arm and tried to yank him backward.

"I hate this cat," Levi said vehemently. "If he pukes in my stuff one more time, I can't be held responsible for my actions."

"What did he puke on now?" I asked, a little freaked out by Levi's intensity. I mean, animal vomit didn't thrill me either, but it was like twenty degrees outside and we were in the school parking lot. He couldn't seriously be that mean as to ditch a defenseless pet out there.

"My jeans. My book bag. My *pillow*."

Okay, that was nasty, but still. "Well, he obviously has some dietary issues. My mom can switch out his food." I hit the button by the driver's seat to close the side door to the van, hoping the cat wouldn't leap out before it shut. I had no interest in tearing across the parking lot in pursuit of Zoe's cat. "Zoe loves this cat, Levi. She sleeps with him."

Levi and the cat were in some kind of staring match.

And Levi's eyes had started to do that freaky red glowing thing that only happened when . . .

Uh-oh.

He only did that when he was in the presence of another demon and they were having a showdown.

Which must mean that Zoe's little ball of fluff so charmingly named, was actually a demon from hell.

I swiveled to check out the cat's smooshed face. Yellow glowing eyes. Check.

"Levi, this cat is a demon!" I shrieked. "Why didn't you tell me?"

"Shh!" he yelled right back. "The girls are here."

He was right. The door whipped open and a pack of girls clamored into the van and started squealing in delight at the sight of the cat.

"How did Marshmallow Pants get in here?" my mom asked with an exhausted sigh.

By the powers of his demonic and furry self. "I don't know."

"We'll have to drop him back at the house. Okay, everyone find a seat!"

Levi shifted to the back, taking the squirming cat with him, and after a lot more chatter, climbing over each other, and cat petting, all four girls were finally buckled in and we were off to the zoo, with a slight detour to drop demon cat off.

I glanced back at Levi sitting next to Dakota, who was clutching Marshmallow Pants with a rapturous expression on her face. Levi was frowning. When he felt my stare and glanced my way, I raised my eyebrow in question.

"What?" he asked.

"Should you let her hold him?" I asked. It seemed a little dicey, you know, letting a five-year-old cling to a creature from hell. Just saying.

He grimaced at me. "You try to take him away."

I wasn't sure if he was saying he didn't want new scratches now that his old ones had finally healed, or if he didn't want Dakota going ballistic on him, so I just reached out and tried to take the cat. "Can I hold him, Dakota?"

The sweet little blonde shot me an evil "die, bitch" look and clung to Marshmallow Pants (by the way, it was getting harder and harder to think of a demon by that candy-coated name) tightly. "No!" she said. "And my name's not Dakota!"

"Well, what is it then?"

"Georgia."

Close enough. I had a state, just the wrong region. "Oh, I'm sorry, Georgia. But can I please have the cat? We need to take him into the house in a minute."

"No."

I swear the kid was actually snarling at me and I didn't like that satanic gleam in her eye. I looked at Levi. "See? This is your fault."

"How is this my fault?"

But of course I couldn't talk about it, because we were surrounded by kindergartners and my mother was in earshot, so I let it ride. I also let Dakota / Georgia keep the cat. It wasn't worth having my eyes scratched out—and that was probably just what the kid would do to me. No telling what the demon might pull.

I sat back and bided my time until we got to the zoo, figuring there would be plenty of opportunities to corner Levi in the cat house and force some answers out of him.

Zoe and her patch-earning pals were giggling and pointing at a bunch of fish up ahead in the aquatics building, so I nudged Levi and gestured for him to hang back. "I need to talk to you."

"I'm a group leader," he informed me, continuing to walk. "I have to stay with Group Four—Alexis, Zoe, Mandy, and Brittany. They're my responsibility."

Best Big Fake Brother of the year.

"Oh, give me a break! You can see all four of them from here." It really annoyed me that my mother, who as a prosecutor put criminals in prison on a biweekly basis, and who oozed suspicion, seemed to think it made sense to trust small children to Levi. Granted, my mother didn't know that Levi was a demon escaped from prison, but all she knew was that Levi had suddenly appeared as my new friend in need of a place to stay, and she had not only swallowed his story of divorcing parents battling it out, she had let him move in and started feeding Levi her appalling casseroles with zero questions.

Now she was entrusting her favorite child to him? It boggled the mind.

"Okay, but if they start moving, we need to follow them," he conceded. "What's up?"

He wasn't even looking at me, but had his eyes fixed on Group 4. I had to begrudgingly admit that was why my CON list had existed at all. Because he always managed to show that despite his annoyingness, he was a good guy, and it was clear then that he took the girls' safety seriously.

"What do you think is up? You just told me that little cute kitten is a demon. What does that mean, exactly? What kind of demon?"

"I never said he was a demon."

"Hello, it was obvious. His eyes were glowing."

"Cats eyes glow."

And so would mine, from fury, if he didn't stop talking in circles. "Are you trying to tell me now that the cat isn't a demon? If you are, save your breath, because I don't believe you."

He sighed. "Fine. You're right."

"What kind of demon is it? A prisoner?"

"No, definitely not a prisoner."

Well, that was reassuring. It still irritated me that of all the demonic portals to open, I had managed to open a prison portal. Like demons weren't bad enough, I had to open the door to the underworld that held the dregs of demon society. Picture that mess.

"Who is it then? And why is it a cat?"

"Not sure." Levi took a step forward like he was going to break into a run, then stopped, dropped his arms, and sighed. "Crap. Mandy almost fell off that step. Watching kids is hard work."

So while he babysat, it was once again up to me to figure everything out when I knew nothing about anything.

Sounded about right for my life.

I stared at a shark hanging out in its tank looking bored out of its gills and thought he and I had a lot in common. He was stuck in a tank that amounted to about the size of a bathtub compared to what he was used to, and I was grounded with no friends.

Feeling a whine coming on, I turned and went to my mother.

"What's wrong, baby?" she asked me, linking her arm through mine. "You look upset."

Sometimes it was nice to have a mother to lean on, even if she was shorter than me.

"I hate Levi," I told her.

She laughed. "Maybe you two should just accept that you want to be a couple."

Gak. So much for Mom Comfort. She was rooting for the wrong team and it felt like a betrayal.

"And where has Isabella been lately?" she asked.

Just turn the knife a little more, Mom.

Chapter Ten

When I got home I Googled the demon Otis. Turned out Otis was a nickname for Botis—you couldn't fault the guy there for trying to make the most out of a crap name like that. Yikes. I sometimes complained that my parents should have just named me Mackenzie since that's what everyone seemed to think my name must be for Kenzie to be my nickname. But it wasn't my nickname, it was my full complete name, and as a result it can't have a nickname generated from it as it sounds like a nickname in and of itself, which made me happy. I didn't want a nickname.

But I would totally go for Otis if I were Botis.

The description of him wasn't even remotely encouraging. "A ruler of hell, he appears on Earth with sharp teeth and a sword." Or as a fluffy white cat. Huh. But when I thought about it, the cat had sharp teeth and the sword could be translated as his claws. He was constantly doing a number on Levi.

Which made more sense now that I understood they knew each other.

Levi said Otis wasn't a prisoner. The portal he had exited from was a prison portal. Ruler of hell . . . Who else was in a prison? Prison guards. Otis was most likely a prison guard, which explained the animosity between him and Levi. And seemed as further evidence why I should stop being a wimp and just send Levi back right along with Otis aka Marshmallow Pants.

Had I ever really gotten any sort of reasonable explanation as to why Levi had been in demon prison in the first place? No. Nope. Levi avoided that question like every other one I asked him.

Feeling eyes on me, I quickly turned. There was no one in the open doorway of my room. Unnerved, I checked out my whole room. I let out a yelp when I realized Otis was lying on the foot of my bed, watching me steadily while he licked his foot.

How long had he been there? I minimized my screen but realized he probably knew exactly what and who I was researching. I had actually read the description of Otis out loud. Heart thumping faster than normal, I gripped the edge of my desk and eyeballed him. "Can I help you?"

He let out a meow, then leaped off my bed. He paused halfway across the carpet and looked at me, like he was waiting for me to follow him. I was so going to regret doing it, but I got up and followed him, wiping my sweaty palms on my jeans. "Where are we going?"

Otis strolled into my bathroom, with its black and aqua blue color scheme and its crisp white towels, and jumped onto the rim of the bathtub. He did a graceful walk back and forth on the shiny, slippery surface, pausing to rub his shoulder on the shower curtain.

"What?" I said. "I don't get it."

He jumped to my counter and knocked over my acne meds—yeah, guess I should have put those away after using—with his nose. Then he jumped back over to the tub edge and stood there meowing, looking down at the drain.

"You want me to open this portal back up?" I asked in shock, when I finally realized what he was trying to tell me without benefit of English skills. "No way! How stupid do I look?"

If a cat could raise an eyebrow, this one did. He just blinked at me, arrogance and disdain dripping from his Marshmallow Pants pores.

"Don't look at me like that. I'm not doing it." I probably shouldn't even be in the bathroom alone with him now that I thought about it.

Otis meowed.

"No."

He jumped behind the shower curtain with a meow that I was pretty sure was a curse.

Great. "What are you doing?" I waited. Nothing happened. I couldn't even hear him moving around.

"Otis. That is your name, right? Come on, I can't understand Cat. I'm sorry. I have no idea what you're saying."

"How about now?" The shower curtain pulled back and I was staring at a dude sitting in my bathtub, knees up to his chin. He was older than Levi, in his twenties, and he had a goatee, sideburns, black eyes, and yellowed fingernails.

You know what I did. Hello. I screamed.

His hand shot up, the bathroom door slammed shut behind me, and he gave me a lecturing, "Shh!"

The door closing scared me into instant silence. I stared at him, breathing heavily, arms across my chest, like that would somehow protect me.

"Open this portal," he demanded. "It's the easiest way for me to go back and take Leviathan with me."

"How did you get here? Can't you go back that way?"

"You know how I got here."

Actually, no I didn't. That's why I was *asking*. "Why are you a cat?"

"Try and explain this," he said, gesturing to himself in human form.

Good point. Not only was he a good five years older than me, he had tattoos from wrist to elbow on both arms, an eyebrow piercing, and a T-shirt with a bleeding skull on it. Probably my mom would not be so happy if I was hanging around with this guy.

"Cat is easier." He smiled, but it wasn't really a happy kind of expression. He sort of looked like he had a fever, his eyes glassy, skin pale. "Most of the time."

"How do I close the air portal?" I asked. Not that he would give me an answer, but hey, it was worth a shot.

"You don't want to close it," he said, shaking his head vehemently. "The only way you're going to be able to fix this breach in underworld security is to open all the portals at once. When you do that, you take their collective energy and shut them down all together. You're the conduit."

I was a conduit. I so didn't want to hear that. I wasn't even sure what it meant frankly, but it sounded like this whole mess revolved around me somehow. Note to self: Look up conduit later when I didn't have a cat demon turned dirty rocker human in my bathtub.

"I don't want to be the conduit."

He actually rolled his eyes. "Who asked you?"

Yet another good point. "And Levi told me I can't have all the portals open at once or the whole thing will open." Leaving West Shore, and in particular my house, open to an infestation of demonic prisoners and their whip-cracking prison guards.

"And did you ever wonder what Levi's motive might be? Or why he's in prison?"

Yes. Frequently. "Why is he in prison?" I asked cautiously.

"Just ask him about Lilith." Otis actually grinned. "See what he tells you."

Lilith? Somehow that sounded like a story I didn't want to hear. Involving star-crossed lovers and the demon he killed for her.

"Why are you in prison?"

"I'm not. I'm a guard. I'm here to take Levi back and to get you to open these portals so you can close them once and for all. We don't like prisoners slipping out."

I wasn't so fond of it either.

"Just think what you might get next time. Levi is harmless, but that's not what might pop out if you leave these portals open."

Like him, maybe? I didn't feel threatened exactly, but Otis was no boy next door. It wasn't hard to picture his eyes glowing and a couple of thick, yellowed horns popping out of that shaggy hair. "So I take it Levi doesn't want to go back and that's why the two of you don't get along?"

"Yes."

"Why don't you just go into human form and drag him back the way you came?" If he was a prison guard, you'd think he'd have strength, training, weaponry. Not that he looked like he was packing heat in his fur when he was in cat form.

The whole thing was insane.

"Aren't you listening to me?" He leaned back, his hands behind his head, and lounged in my tub. "I can't do it without you, little girl."

I blinked. Did he just call me little girl? How creepy was that?

There was a knock on my door. "Kenzie?" It was Levi. "Who are you talking to?"

Otis met my questioning look with a steady stare, shaking his head no. I turned to the door. "The cat," I said. When I looked back, Otis was back to being Marshmallow Pants, licking the drain.

I opened the door and met Levi's worried look with a fake smile. "What do you need?"

He pushed past me. "Why are you in here with the cat?"

"Because I had to go to the bathroom and he followed me in here. I guess he wanted a drink from the drain."

Levi pulled Otis out of the bathtub, holding him out to avoid the claws that were trying to swipe him, and said, "Don't ever do that, Kenzie."

"Do what?" I watched him dump Otis into the hallway.

"Go to the bathroom, change your clothes, take a shower in front of this cat."

"Because he's a demon."

"Yes."

"Well, I didn't, because now I know he's a demon, but I didn't know that yesterday. Thanks for looking out for me then." I racked my brain to remember if I might have ever changed clothes in front of Otis, but I couldn't remember any particular instances. The thought of Otis walking around—down low, by the way— watching me gave me the heebies. And I seriously didn't like the fact that he was hanging with my baby sister, even if it was in cat form.

"I couldn't."

"I know. Demon rules. Whatever." I had heard it all. "And who is Lilith?"

Levi's face drained of color. "Lilith? What do you know about Lilith?"

"Nothing. Just her name, and that she probably has something to do with the fact that you were in prison."

The color all ran back into his face and he turned red from rage. "Otis shifted into human form?"

"Just for a minute. Long enough to tell me to ask you about Lilith and that I should open all five portals at once if I want to then close them."

"I'll kill him. I'm really going to kill him," Levi said. "Don't listen to a single thing he says, do you understand? He'll lie and try to trick you into doing what he wants."

Like anyone else I knew?

"He wants all the portals open so he can claim credit for it. He's the prison warden."

Oh, so now we elevated Otis from mere guard to warden?

I couldn't keep up.

Underworld politics was wearing me out.

"I can't even close one portal, why would I be stupid enough to open all five at once then try to close them? I'm not a moron, Levi." Even though everyone seemed to think I was.

He didn't answer, which irritated me. He did think I was a moron? But I realized he probably hadn't even heard me since he was leaving the room, eyes darting left and right.

"Otis, where are you?"

They were going to have a demon smackdown. This could get ugly.

I could hear Zoe reprimanding from the family room. "Stop calling him that, Levi! His name is *Marshmallow Pants*."

Which I'm sure just thrilled a prison warden.

I decided maybe I needed to have a little chat with Zoe about leaving the hot pink onesies on the baby dolls and off the cat from hell. I'd seen the human side he'd chosen and he didn't really look like he was in touch with his softer side. One more bonnet and yellow sundress just might send him over the edge.

Downstairs Levi was holding his hands out and pleading with Zoe. "Just let me see the cat, Zoe."

"No!" Zoe had Otis in her lap and was brushing his fur, with about zero gentleness. The cat's head was actually flinging back with each pass through of the brush, which looked suspiciously like Zoe's own hairbrush. Where was my mother and her hyperhygiene when you needed it?

My dad wandered into the room with a bag of potato chips. Despite my mom's harassing, he has horrible eating habits, yet still manages to stay thin. I was fortunate enough to get that awesome little gene from him because I was all about the dairy products.

"What's going on?" he asked, raising a chip to his lips.

"The cat needs a bath," Levi said.

Yeah, like a dunk in the lake with rocks tied around his paws, if Levi had anything to do with it.

"He does not," Zoe insisted.

"He stinks like garbage and he killed another mouse. I found it in my gym bag."

And Levi didn't look happy about it.

It occurred to me it was no coincidence Levi was on the receiving end of all of Marshmallow Pants's little gifts of rodent carcasses and cat food vomit. It might be intimidation, but more likely it was just a demonic joke.

My dad grimaced. "I paid two hundred bucks to the exterminator and we still have mice? I'm going to call them and make them redo the spraying."

It always came down to the wallet with dad. He glanced over at me. "When did you dye your hair red?"

"Only the tips and it was like two weeks ago. You need to keep up, Dad." And I needed to get that cat away from Zoe. Otis was starting to hiss at her as her combing got more and more aggressive.

"Come on, Zoe. We'll give MP a bath together. We'll do it in the laundry room." How hard could bathing a cat be? I reached out and picked the cat up. Otis came willingly, and actually snuggled up against my chest, his head right along my . . .

Ack. I dropped the cat back onto the couch with zero hesitation. Perv. I swear he was actually smiling up at me as he realized I realized exactly what he was doing. I also decided I didn't want to wash his fluffy butt after all. He would probably enjoy it.

"Actually, I have homework. Levi can do it with you."

Levi glared at me and I realized he had never intended to actually give the cat a bath. He just wanted to get him away from Zoe.

"That cat still has all four claws," Dad said. "There is no way any of us can give him a bath without losing an eye. If he really smells that bad we'll have to take him to the groomer's and they can sedate him and do it." He winced. "Yet another expense."

Leaving Levi to deal with it, I opened the kitchen drawer and pulled out the dictionary.

Conduit. 1: a channel for conveying fluid.

Eew. How disgusting sounding was that? Please tell me I would not be conveying any fluids any time soon. Ever.

2: a tube or trough for protecting electric wires or cables.

Next. I was no tube or trough either.

3: a means of transmitting or distributing.

Okay, that was probably what Otis had meant. I made the transmission of demons from the prison to my house possible.

Now I just needed to figure out how to stop doing that. Immediately if not sooner.

Chapter Eleven

Logic didn't have a chance in my life.

It was time to just accept that little fact and move on.

Anyone else could have done what I did (I had the urge to scream in the halls at school, *It was just a kiss, it was only a kiss!*) and it would be no biggie. Everyone would forget in like a minute and life would go on.

Not me.

Isabella still wasn't talking to me, Adam still wasn't talking to me, the entire school still wasn't talking to me, and I was getting used to eating lunch while listening to my iPod and planning my escape from public school and entrance into performing arts school. I would have to drug my parents to get them to sign the application, but I figured that was a small price to pay to reclaim some small piece of happiness in my life.

Levi sometimes tried to sit with me at lunch, but I had the feeling that would be a bad idea and only make me look guilty, so I usually blew him off.

But Monday he actually sat down at my empty table with Amber Jansen. I wondered what he had promised her (engagement ring, anyone?) to get her to agree to sit with me, but she did it. With a fake smile on her face even. Impressive.

"This is a fun twist," I said.

"Well, the way everyone is treating you just totally sucks," Levi said. "So I figured if Amber sat with you, and everyone saw that she, of all people, is cool with you, and cool with you and I being friends, that everyone else would get a grip and let it go."

I wasn't sure that the plan would work at all, but I appreciated the effort. "Thanks, Amber," I said, and I didn't even choke on the words. I actually meant it. "I appreciate it."

"Sure," she said, her smile almost snapping in half.

"Look, just so you know, Levi and I . . . we aren't . . . we didn't . . . we don't want to be together." Yeah, I was so making things better. Not. "I mean, what I'm trying to say is you can trust us. Levi wants to be with you and I think that's awesome. It's the way it should be. You're a great couple."

Who was speaking? I couldn't believe the words coming out of my mouth even as I said them, but then again, spending day after day in total silence was enough to make anyone go completely insane. I was willing to say whatever I had to to get at least one friend back. One friend that wasn't Levi, that is. And there was truth to what I was saying. Levi and I had never discussed our second little kiss (well, okay, not so little), and it was pretty clear we were going to ignore it forever and he was going to be with Amber.

"Okay, Kenzie," she said, shoving her fork around her bare salad. Who ate a salad with no dressing? Yuck.

"Just quit while you're ahead," she added.

It probably wouldn't help my cause if I stuck my tongue out at her, so I managed to restrain myself.

At least when I got home every day I could count on the attention and devotion of Mike, the nineteen-year-old construction worker who had an amazing collection of holey T-shirts. I had never seen him wear the same one twice.

Mike was good after-school company, despite the fact that we had trouble understanding each other. He tended to talk football and electric saws, and I tended to speak in theater analogies. So we did a lot of "What does that mean?" with each other. But I would have listened to a piece of moldy cheese if it had been willing to talk to me, I was so bored with my own company.

The only upside of my social situation was there was no way my dad would give his usual threats and lectures when my cell phone bill arrived. I was going to be under my minutes. By about all of them.

Anyway, Mike kept me company, and I was sure he wasn't a demon, because why would he put up with his dad and uncle if he was? He would just vanquish them or something and live life off the demon bank the way Levi did. Or he could demon mojo his way into a cool job, like movie critic or something.

So he obviously wasn't a demon and had no idea that the busted-up kitchen wall he was helping to repair contained an open air portal. I wished I didn't know anything about it either. Wait. I didn't.

I did wonder if when they fixed the wall, the portal would just automatically close by itself, but that seemed way optimistic. When did anything in my life ever just go away? Exactly. Never.

Which lead me to think that when they sealed that sucker up, they would actually be leaving an open air portal in the wall, with no way for me to access it to close it. It also seemed to me that the only way to get rid of air (aside from vacuuming it, which so hadn't worked) was to displace it. Move it out of the way with an object. Plug it. Fill the space. Give the air nowhere to go.

It all made sense to me with my limited science knowledge. Note that I should have been in chemistry by junior year but wasn't because I was on a slow track (aka don't give the scientifically and mathematically challenged students chemicals to play with). So really, it's not like I knew what I was doing and I had no reason to trust myself on this one, but I had to do *something*. I wanted life to go back to normal.

So I asked Mike, "How long until you're done here? It doesn't look any different to me than when you started." It was still a hole.

"We'll be done by the end of the week," he said. "We're done

138

with framing, electrical, and plumbing. Just need insulation, then drywall."

Did he look sad to be leaving me? Or was that just the wishful thinking of a desperate teen without friends or a driver's license?

My dad had decided to upgrade the wiring since the wall was blown open, so the cool thing to come out of my little accident that wasn't an accident was that we would now have better wireless access, an intercom system, and an iPod docking station in the kitchen cabinet. Everyone had me to thank for that.

"Oh. So then you move on to the next project?"

"Yep." He was cleaning up for the day, sweeping up the sawdust and shifting the industrial fan they used out of the way. His father and uncle had left for the day already and he was stuck finishing up. "You sure you can't go out with me?" he asked, looking hopeful.

I pictured floating that one past my father. "I can ask, but I'm pretty sure my parents will laugh hysterically in my face before they say no."

"Just ask. You never know."

"Okay." What did I have to lose, really? And while it wasn't like I had any sort of burning desire to date Mike (that had been reserved for Adam) I did like him now that I knew he wasn't a serial killer, and what else did I have going on?

"Cool. I have to unload the insulation out of my truck into the garage. Stick around, okay?"

I pushed myself off the island where I had been leaning. "I can help you."

Mike looked dubious. "You don't have to do that. It's heavy."

Heavy? Yeah, I was out. "Well, I can try. And if I can't lift it, which is highly probable, I can talk to you while you do it."

I tripped over the fan cord on my way around the island. Have I mentioned how graceful I am?

"Whoa, careful." Mike reached out and steadied me.

Tripping was a daily adventure for me, so I just laughed. "I didn't fall. That's a good sign." I plugged the fan back in, and because I'm random I turned it on just to see how industrial it really was. The turbo fan was so strong my eyeballs instantly dried out and my hair shot straight backward.

"Whoa."

"What are you doing?" Mike watched me with a small smile.

"Look. I'm a model." I did mock poses, simpering and pouting as the fan blew my hair. Spinning a few times, I wound up doing the Charleston. Signs of a truly bored individual.

But Mike laughed and reached out and grabbed my hand. It was the first time he'd really ever touched me and I was shocked at how big his hand was. Mine looked like a toddler's swimming in his. He pulled me to the garage and I suddenly had the feeling that retrieving insulation was going to result in a kiss in the garage. I wasn't sure how I felt about that. I liked Mike, but I didn't *like* him, and I didn't really want to lead him on. Plus a little harmless kiss was responsible for my current situation. Another one with another guy seemed like it might complicate things even more and result in both parental and Levi anger.

On the other hand, why should I care if Levi was mad at me?

We couldn't get along for three minutes anyway. And maybe my going out with Mike would make him jealous.

Not that I cared.

It didn't matter to me what Levi thought.

And it so wasn't true that I was jealous of him being with Amber.

Nope.

So I let Mike lead me outside into the garage and down the driveway to his truck. "Ugh, it's cold out here," I said, shivering and flipping up the hood on my hoodie.

"It's not too bad." Mike was only wearing a T-shirt and he had no goose bumps and didn't look the slightest bit uncomfortable. Clearly he was meant to live in northern Ohio, while I should have been born in the Caribbean. If I had, I would have been wearing a bikini on the beach instead of shivering in my driveway wondering if I would ever survive February if November was already doing me in.

He reached into his truck and handed me a nylon jacket. "Put this on."

I did. And it ate me.

The sleeves went to my knees and the bottom of the jacket hit my ankles, I swear. It was so heavy, my shoulders strained to stay upright. It smelled like cologne, though just faintly, nowhere near Dirk Danger levels.

While I screwed around adjusting the jacket and shoving up the sleeves, Mike was hauling bags of stuff back and forth. I was so very helpful as usual. Making an effort, I tried to reach into the truck bed and grab a bag, but that was as far as it got. I tugged and pulled, but I couldn't make it move. Guess construction was out for me as a future career choice, as if anyone could have ever pictured me in a hard hat. I went and stood in the garage and pestered Mike with questions since I had the strength of an ant. Of course, ants carry giant—relative to themselves—crumbs over their heads for long distances, so the truth was I was probably weaker than just about any living creature.

"This isn't the roll of insulation. What is this stuff?"

"It's the kind you blow in, like snowflakes. We discovered that the attic space above the garage here isn't insulated, so your dad wants some blown in."

"You blow it in? Cool." I sat on a bag of the stuff and thought that one through while Mike went back and forth.

Huh. Blow-in insulation. Displace the air.

Do you see where my brain was going with this?

"Show me how it works," I said. Maybe if he showed me how to do it, I could sneak down after my parents were in bed and fill up the wall.

Unsupervised was probably a bad idea, though.

I'd just do it with Mike. Right then and there. Why not, right?

"You want to see how it works? Why?"

"Curiosity. It amazes me how you know so much." Gag. I heard my own sugar-sweet voice and almost threw up in my mouth. I was now cheapening myself just to close this stupid portal and that made me mad. This seriously needed to stop. I wanted to be done with the whole demon thing once and for all.

Mike didn't question my sincerity at all, he just started explaining to me how the whole process worked. I tried to listen, I really did, but he lost me after "ninety-seven percent radiant energy."

I tuned back in when he held up a spray can–looking kind of thing.

"So then you just aim and spray," he said.

That was all I needed to know. "Is it loaded now?"

"Yep."

"Let me see." I stood up and faced the hole in the wall. I was just going to do this thing. Spray it. No thinking, no hesitation. Just do it. Win.

Or lose.

"Don't push the—" Mike said.

Too late. I pushed the button and feathery insulation flew out at the hole in the wall. Which would have been cool, fine, all good. Except it hit the industrial-strength fan I had turned on in the kitchen. The fan that was pointed right at the hole. Which shot straight back into the garage a million white flakes that went right into my face.

I screamed, startled and blinded by all that white suddenly blocking my vision. Mike was yelling for me to turn it off and I could feel his fingers groping around to yank the dispenser away from me, but I panicked and didn't let go as it nailed me in the face, the eyes, went up my nose, and got into my mouth.

Stumbling backward, I felt my right foot slip on something. My arms flailed in the too-big jacket, and I did the splits, hovering for one beautiful moment between safety and disaster. Then I went down like a bowling pin.

Just an FYI for you, a garage floor is hard.

I dropped the insulation blower thing and turned to brace my fall out of instinct. Pain shot through my hip and my arm when I made contact with the concrete, and I just lay there for a second on the cold floor, stunned, catching my breath and making sure all my parts were still attached.

"Are you okay?" Mike hovered over me.

"Ow," I said. "I hurt my arm." It hurt bad. Really bad. Really, really bad.

I have this charming habit of throwing up when I'm in pain, so I turned and hurled in the opposite direction of Mike's feet. He let out a surprised "Whoa!" as my stomach clenched and heaved. Laying my face back down on the concrete after I lost my after-school snack, I took deep breaths and tried to relax through the pain.

That didn't work.

And that was when I saw the rotting, gelatinous apple peel on the floor in front of me. *That* was what I had slipped on?

It figured.

Mike swore and squatted down beside me. "Here, I'm going to help you up. Is it just your arm?"

I lay there and wiggled all my parts and reflected. "Yeah." It was just my arm sending shooting pain out in all directions. Funny how one little limb could make my whole body clench in agony. My cell phone buzzed in my hoodie pocket, letting me know I had a text. "I have a text message," I said stupidly.

"Are your parents home?" he asked.

"No, they're not home from work yet. My brother and sister are here. And maybe Levi. And the cat."

"I don't think a five-year-old or a cat are going to be much help."

He had no idea what that cat was possibly capable of, but I wasn't going to enlighten him.

Mike got behind me and helped me into a sitting position.

It was definitely better than lying on the freezing floor, but my arm twisted when I sat up and I sucked in some air. "Oh, dude, this kills . . ." Tears ran down my face even as I thought I should try to be tough.

Then I realized tough and Kenzie don't belong in the same sentence. "Ow, ow, ow . . ." I moaned pitifully.

"Let me have your cell phone," Mike said. "I'm going to call your parents and have them meet us at the ER."

Good, solid plan. It was a good thing someone was rational, because all I was thinking was that it might be better to just lie back down on the floor and wait to die.

"It's in my hoodie pocket."

Mike dug around in my clothes in a way that might have either weirded me out or excited me under different circumstances, but he emerged with my black skull-sticker-decorated cell.

"Are your parents just listed as Mom and Dad or what?" he asked, scrolling through my contacts list.

"I don't know." I was having focus issues. All I could think was that nothing in my entire life had ever hurt that bad and that if I moved even one inch, I just might throw up again.

"This text is from Levi . . . Do you want to read it?"

I almost told him to just read it, but I decided that could be potentially embarrassing. "Yeah, sure." One-handed, I took the phone and read Levi's charming as usual text.

Where r u?

Garage, I typed back, then handed the phone back to Mike, all queased out from the effort. "Oh, I feel sick again."

"Just take a deep breath. I'm going to call your mom, because you have Mom listed here, and then we'll get you into my truck. We can be at the ER in less than ten minutes, and they'll fix you right on up."

He was very calm and I definitely appreciated that. As he pushed Send and waited for my mother to pick up her cell, he even brushed insulation flakes off my face, lips, and uninjured shoulder. He was smart enough to leave the left one I had hurt alone.

And he managed to inform my mother what was going on efficiently and without drama, suggesting she meet us at the ER as soon as possible.

There was something to be said for blowing insulation in your face and snapping your arm in the presence of a nineteen-year-old who was gainfully employed. He was handling the crisis, which was good, because I was just fighting the urge to puke again and picking out my cast color. My arm just had to be broken given the way it felt, and frankly, if it wasn't, I was going to feel cheated. Only broken bones should hurt that much.

Mike got behind me. "Okay, I'm going to help you stand up. Then we'll get you in the truck and I'll check to make sure your brother or Levi is here to stay with your sister."

Oh, yeah. The five-year-old. Had totally forgotten about her. Sister of the Year Award would not be given to me.

Good thing Mike was used to hauling lumber and insulation and whatever else, because I was like spaghetti and couldn't even get my own legs to push me up off the ground. But no problem. He just got me around the waist and hauled me straight up.

"You okay?"

He was still gripping me around the waist, and I was limping leaning against him holding my arm gingerly in front of my chest when I heard, "What are you doing?"

I half turned and saw Levi standing in the doorway. He strode over to us, looking all sorts of horrified and annoyed.

"I fell," I told him.

"I think she broke her arm. I'm taking her to the ER."

Levi's expression changed to concerned. "Are you okay?" he asked, scanning me head to toe.

"No, I'm not. I broke my arm and I'm going to the ER." Didn't Mike just say that?

"Okay, I'll take you."

"It's cool," Mike said. "I'm taking her. I already called her mom."

"I could have called your mom," Levi said to me, as if Mike didn't even exist.

Oh, I so didn't need the possessive thing under the current circumstances. I just looked at him, hoping my face conveyed that I wished a portal would open up and swallow him. "I'm sure you could have if you had been the one standing here when I fell. But it was Mike who was standing here when I fell, and we've got it covered, thanks. I need you to stay here with Zoe."

"Right, okay, sure, of course. Call me and let me know how you're doing." Levi glanced around and frowned. "What is all this white crap?"

The remains of another one of my brilliant ideas.

Chapter Twelve

I chose black.

"I'm not surprised," my mother said as we got out of the mini-van, my arm in its new cast and sling. "But I was hopeful you'd pick the hot pink or even the cherry red."

"I broke my arm, Mom. My mood is black, therefore my cast is black." And that way no one could see that I would not be getting my cast covered in signatures and pictures because I was still a social outcast at West Shore High.

"Well, at least that nice boy Mike was here to see that you . . . What the . . ." My mother looked around the garage in bewilderment. "What is all this mess?"

Oh, yeah. I had forgotten she'd missed the snowball effect of my attempt to close the portal with insulation flakes. "I accidentally sprayed the insulation thing. It hit me in the eye, which is how I tripped and fell."

My mother stared hard at me. "Why do I think there is more to that story than you're telling me?"

"What?" I blinked innocently at her. "It was just me being a curious klutz, touching what I shouldn't have. It was totally all my fault."

Her eyebrow went up. "Now I know there's more to it if you're taking responsibility so easily."

How rude, if accurate. Time for a diversion. I winced. "Ow. My arm really hurts. Can I go sit down?"

She went from suspicious to worried in 1.2 seconds flat. "Of course, baby."

When I went in the house Zoe was bouncing around all excited to see my injury. Her little hands came out for my cast and I stumbled back three feet. "Don't touch it! It hurts!" I pictured her grabbing on and twisting in enthusiasm to inspect the cast, and my arm ached just in horrified anticipation.

It really did hurt anyway from all the X-raying and pressing and wrapping. The last thing I needed was Zoe's grubby hands knocking me around. Lucky me, I had a compound fracture in my arm and a broken wrist (two for the price of one) so I had the full cast from knuckles to elbow and bent like I had been frozen solid while doing a backup dance move for a pop video. It was awful and heavy and I wanted Tylenol and a quiet corner to cry in.

I settled for flopping on the couch, which made my arm bounce and pain shoot through it. "Argh." My arm had nowhere to go and just dangled in the sling in the air, tormenting me. I tried to reach the remote and almost lost my balance so I just gave up and stared sullenly into space.

Good times ahead, clearly.

Levi jumped up and inserted a pillow between my thigh and the cast so that my arm had somewhere to rest. He handed me the remote and bent over really close to me. "Hey. You okay?"

"No." I frowned up at him. "But thanks," I added sullenly.

"What were you doing?" he asked quietly.

"Nothing."

"That guy is too old for you."

"Thanks, Dad."

"I'm serious, K. He's out of high school."

"I'm aware of that."

"Your parents will freak."

"I know." I pushed his chest. "Will you back up? I can't breathe."

"Promise me you won't go out with him."

Annoyed, I decided not to enlighten him that I had really no intention of going out with Mike. I had realized that while Mike was an incredibly nice guy, we really did have zero in common and he actually deserved someone who was really into him, not me, who was only interested out of sheer boredom. I may be a klutz, but I am not selfish—well, not ultimately. We're all somewhat selfish, right? And I'm no exception, but I wasn't mean.

Well, maybe except when it came to refusing to reassure Levi, who was clearly worried about me. I was all prepared to tell him that I couldn't make any promises where love was concerned, when my conscience got the best of me.

"I'm not going out with him. Now leave me alone."

He looked altogether too pleased with that answer, making me regret my decision to be nice.

Just once it might be fun to watch him writhe in agony.

Showing up at school with a cast that prevented me from bending my arm (hello, half my wardrobe wouldn't even fit over the stupid thing) and was ink black got me attention I wasn't expecting.

People started talking to me again, and even if it was just out of morbid curiosity, I was prepared to take it. I didn't even remind repeating for the tenth time that I had fallen in the construction zone of my garage. No way was I admitting I had actually slipped on a rotting satanic apple skin. Though chances were no one would believe that. It was hard to believe myself.

At lunch, I balanced my tray with my good hand when I got to my empty table in the corner and tried to pull the chair out with my foot. My backpack swung dangerously on my back and I had visions of it slamming forward, knocking me and my tray onto the table.

Suddenly there was another hand on the tray, steadying it and preventing total disaster. I glanced over and the "Thanks" froze in my throat. It was Isabella.

"Do I even want to know how you broke your arm?" she

asked, removing the tray entirely from my grip and setting it down on the table.

"You know me," I said, feeling a flicker of hope. "I slipped in a cloud of insulation flakes in my garage. Went down with zero grace. Years of dance training wasted on me . . . I can't even walk without hurting myself."

"I'm sorry," she said. "It must kill."

"It does. And the director of *Midsummer Night's Dream* is not going to be thrilled with me. We'll have to redo my costume." Then because I didn't want her to walk away, I said, "Iz, I'm totally sorry for what happened at the party. I didn't mean to hurt you . . . that's the last thing I would ever want. Levi just caught me off guard. I should have told him to go to hell but I didn't, and I really am sorry."

I really did need to learn how to tell Levi to go to hell. Or go back to hell. I was having issues with that, I had to admit.

Holding my breath, I waited for her to say something, anything.

She sighed. "It still sucks that you didn't, but the thing is, I don't think a guy and thirty seconds should come between us and five years of friendship."

Yes. I let out my breath with a whoosh. "Me either. I miss you."

She sat down at the table. "So you want to go out Friday night? I've been bored out of my mind without you to hang with."

"I'm still grounded." I sat down across from her and tried to open my juice bottle one-handed. "But you can come over and we can watch DVDs and stalk people on MySpace."

"Cool." Isabella ripped the juice bottle out of my hand and uncapped it. "Dude, you're totally helpless, aren't you? How long do you have to wear that thing?"

"Six freaking weeks."

"That sucks."

"Seriously. But I only have one more week to my grounding sentence. One more weekend at home and one more Daisy Girl Scout meeting, then I'm done." In the nick of time too. If I had to look at my brother's filthy laundry one more time, I was going to surgically remove my eyes. "What's new with you?"

"Nothing." Isabella shrugged. "Oh, look, here's your new lunch buddies to join us." Her tone of voice left no doubt as to her feelings about that.

I looked up and stifled a sigh myself. Levi and Amber were heading our way. Sometimes I wondered if Levi had been sent to prison solely for being the deadly triple combination of annoying, persistent, and clueless.

"Hey," I said.

Levi plunked his food right on down next to me, forcing Amber to sit next to Isabella or risk looking like a total freak by sitting next to Levi and having us lined up all on one side of the table. Why did Amber put up with Levi? Honestly. I liked to think I wouldn't be that eager for any guy's company that I would be willing to be dragged around and forced to hang out with the chick my boyfriend had kissed while we were still dating.

Hello. Awkward.

Did everyone understand this except for Levi??

Apparently.

"Hey, K. After lunch, I'll carry your backpack to your next class. It's too heavy for you like that, and Amber and I have to pass your science class on our way to health."

Have Levi and Amber deposit me at my next class? Like one big walking weird relationship? What were we, Mormon? "I'm fine."

"No, I've got it."

I had to spell it out for him. "Levi. Adam is in my next class. If you walk me there with Amber, I will never speak to you again for the rest of my life. I will wish painful things on you. I will tell my mother that your parents want you back and you'll have to move out of our house. I will hack into your cell phone account and change your plan to pay per text."

He raised an eyebrow and gave me a look of bewildered hurt. "Fine, geez. Chill out. Just trying to help. That's all I'm ever trying to do."

Amber snorted.

Interesting. Trouble in the paradise of our homecoming king and queen?

That was probably inevitable.

And I shouldn't grin about it.

Really. I shouldn't.

So I smirked instead.

When I sat down at my lab table in Anatomy and Physiology after lunch, I kicked my backpack under my chair and tried to figure out where to put my arm. It hurt if I set it on the table because it was too high, but if I left it in my lap, it was dangling. I needed a pillow, but I didn't seem to have one handy.

Sitting next to Adam in class had been a blast and a half for the last two weeks since the party. It was forty minutes of torture every day trying not to look at him, touch him, or make any sort of eye contact.

But not only did he look at me today, he actually spoke to me. "What happened to your arm?"

Was that concern on his face?

Yeah, that's what I was taking it as. Total concern.

"Oh, I slipped on the insulation stuff they're using in our kitchen remodel and broke my arm." I shrugged like it was no big deal and that I hadn't cried or whined or felt heinously sorry for myself.

"That sucks. Does it hurt?"

I risked a look at him from under my eyelashes. Still looking concerned (yay). "A little," I said, my voice suddenly breathless. I so wanted him to warm up to me again. Even if we were never together, I couldn't stand not speaking. It was miserable and I really didn't like the idea that he was going to hate me for eternity.

"Full cast, huh?" His finger touched the cast over my wrist. "Black. Figures." And he gave me a smile, like we shared a private joke because he knew me and wasn't at all surprised that I had picked a black cast.

"I know. Big shocker." I smiled.

He smiled back, even bigger.

And we might have gotten further than that, like to the point where our eyes met, the world receded, imaginary singers appeared over our heads and sang about the brilliance of our attraction while dancers did the samba, and for one moment, that crystal clear moment when time stood still, we would know that this was It. That we were meant to be together.

Except all of that was stopped before it ever had a chance to even begin by our teacher's slapping a stack of papers down on our lab table and saying, "You two failed your fetal pig dissection. See me after class."

How romantic was that?

I was dancing across the kitchen, unperturbed by the fact that I'd had to take the bus home because as usual Levi had soccer practice and couldn't drive me.

Isabella was talking to me.

Adam was talking to me.

Amber was miserable.

All was right in my world.

Okay, so I had no driver's license still, but with a broken arm I couldn't drive anyway, so why did it matter? Yes, I still had a demonic cat running around my house, but as soon as I figured out how to close the portal, I was sending his furry butt back.

I was almost ungrounded and I could probably get some new clothes out of the broken arm deal since half my clothes wouldn't go on over the cast.

Adam and I had to redo our pig dissection after school on Thursday, but since my arm was out of commission, that meant Adam would have to wield the scalpel and I would have to record our findings. Cool by me because I did not want to slice dead pig flesh yet again. And think of the bonding potential for us. By the time we got to the lower intestines, maybe Adam and I would be back on as West Shore's Most Unlikely Couple.

Mike glanced over at me, his arms full of a giant sheet of drywall that he was holding in place while his uncle nailed it to the wall. "You look happy today—your arm wasn't broken?"

I held my cast up over the kitchen island so he could see it. "Majorly broken. Arm and wrist. I'm an overachiever. Thanks for all your help. I know I was a huge wimp."

"Hey, it hurt, I'm sure. I'm sorry you slipped. I should have been more careful when I was showing you the equipment."

"No, it was my fault."

"It was both of your faults," Mike's dad commented.

Um, because we asked him?

"We're going to be done here by the end of the week," Mike said. "It goes fast once we get to drywall stage. Did you talk to your mom?"

Ooh. Moral dilemma. I could lie and say I did and she said no, I couldn't go out with Mike. Or I could just tell him the truth, that I didn't want to go out with him after all because my life was complicated enough.

Or I could go ask her for real and trust that she would stay true to maternal form and laugh in the face of my dating a nineteen-year-old.

"I'll ask her right now," I said, going with Option C. Mom would get me off the hook. Not the most mature way to handle it, but why make life difficult or hurt someone's feelings if I didn't have to?

I went to dig my cell phone out of my purse and called my mom, knowing that she was probably winding her day down and wouldn't get annoyed that I was calling her at work.

She asked seventy-five questions about my arm and my day and then finally seemed to realize I might actually have a reason for calling. "Did you need something, sweetie?"

"Can I go out on a date Friday night with Mike, our construction worker?"

"The construction worker?" She sounded appalled, which was a good start. "How old is he?"

"Nineteen. You said he was a nice boy." Throw her own words back at her. That was a way to absolutely guarantee she would say no. I moved farther into the family room, over by the TV Zoe had blaring with cartoons. For whatever reason I didn't want Mike overhearing my conversation.

"He is a nice boy. For doing construction on my kitchen and being nice enough to drive my accident-prone daughter to the ER. That doesn't mean I don't think he's way too old to date my accident-prone daughter."

Accident-prone was a slight exaggeration. "I'm sixteen!" I

said, because that seemed fun and dramatic to throw out at her. "And I'm a junior. I'm almost seventeen." In five months, because again, it had a good whiny quality to the declaration.

"Which is still too young to date a man who has his own apartment."

He had his own apartment? Was she serious? That was kind of cool. For a second I almost changed my mind, then I came to my senses. I did not want to date Mike. "Mom. Come on. He's not really that old. He can't even buy alcohol." And why was I still arguing with her? Maybe because it was actually kind of fun when I had no emotional stake in the outcome.

"I'm not kidding, Kenzie. The answer is no. And would you really even be interested if you and Adam hadn't broken up?"

"No. Because I would still be with Adam." Wasn't that like completely obvious? My enjoyment of the conversation disappeared. I wanted to still be with Adam and that wasn't exactly looking likely, despite our finally breaking our lab partner silence.

"So don't just go out with someone to be with someone."

I sighed. "Fine. You already said no anyway. Spare me the 'get to know yourself before you get into another relationship' lecture."

My mom actually laughed. "I don't think I know that lecture. I'll have to practice it first and get back to you."

"Do us both a favor and don't bother. Okay, I'm going to go and tell Mike that my dictatorial mother will not let me go out with a guy who is a whole whopping two years older than me."

"Okay." She didn't sound the least bit concerned at being

labeled a maternal Hitler. Given that she was a prosecutor, she was probably used to it. "Tell him it's nothing personal and I'll see you in an hour, sweetie."

I went back to the kitchen. "Mike, my mom said no. She said you're old enough to have your own apartment."

Mike looked at me, bewildered. "Why does that matter?"

"I know, I had the same reaction. But it means no, I can't go out with you." Because my mom was picturing me, Mike, an empty apartment, and her suddenly finding herself a grandmother.

"Well, that sucks."

Maybe. Maybe not. I wasn't entirely sure.

But I did know that I was checking things off my "Get Kenzie's Life in Order" list. Deal with Mike had been number four after:

- Make up with Isabella. Check.

- Get Adam to actually look at me. Check.

- Eat lunch with Amber. (Okay, this was sarcasm. I didn't really want to do anything with Amber, ever.) But check anyway.

All four done. I could take a certain satisfaction in that.

Marshmallow Pants rubbed up against my leg while I dug one-handed through the pantry looking for a snack. I glared down at him, unnerved by the idea that Otis in human form was squished into that cat and had his cheek all over my calf. "Get off my leg."

It was a reminder that next up after Mike on the list were the biggies:

- Close the portal.

- Send Otis (Marshmallow Pants) back to hell.

- Levi.

Do what with Levi, I had no idea. But do . . . something with him.

The memory of our kiss suddenly smashed into my brain.

Ack. I didn't want to do that with him.

Did I?

No. No, no, no. Of course not.

Chapter Thirteen

It was amazing how long I could ignore the portal when everything was status quo. I let three more days slide by and pretended it didn't exist. At all. Marshmallow Pants was just a fluffy white cat with a digestion problem and Levi was a real boy, à la Pinocchio.

I was not a demon slayer and I had broken my arm spraying insulation, not slipping on a growling apple peel.

It was all good.

Until the cat morphed on me again on Thursday.

I was in the kitchen trying to pretend that the fixing of the kitchen wall meant nothing and that when Mike and company strolled out on Friday at five o'clock, wall freshly painted and ready for my mother to hang her framed print of peaches back up, it didn't mean the portal was still open and inaccessible.

Nope. Wasn't going to think about that.

My mother had picked me up after school since her meeting was canceled and it was hard for me to take the bus with my backpack and jumbo cast. Okay, it wasn't that hard, really, but why turn down a sympathy ride that didn't involve hard seats, wet floors, and the off-key singing of Brad Feldman to his iPod?

I was trying to do my math homework at the kitchen island, but between final construction touches going on behind me and Zoe's fighting with Dakota/Georgia in the family room over a Bratz doll, I was having trouble concentrating.

"Zoe! Let her have the doll. She's your guest," I yelled, hoping they would shut up. It was getting violent in there by the couch, with Zoe clinging to the big-lipped doll, and Dakota/Georgia stumbling around with an armful of Marshmallow Pants.

"No! She had her yesterday. It's my turn."

"You never share," Dakota/Georgia accused. "I'm telling."

"I don't care," Zoe said crankily. "And you need to give me my cat back."

Mike shot me a look of amusement. I wasn't finding it so funny.

"Trade each other the cat and the doll for ten minutes," I said, thinking if I had to get up and go in there I was going to understand where my mother's Mom tone of total irritation came from.

Staring down at my geometry, I didn't wait to see if they initiated fair trade or not. Until I heard a shriek and the low wail of tears starting up.

I glanced up and immediately stumbled down off my stool at what I saw. Problem. Hair, doll, and fur were all flying in the living room.

My baby sister was in a smackdown with her best friend over a Bratz doll and our demonic cat.

"Zoe! Georgia!" They were grappling with each other, tugging and smacking and shoving. Wow. Five-year-olds gone wild and it so wasn't pretty.

I gave up on doing proofs and went to bust up the family room brawl. They both needed to get a grip. Today Bratz dolls, tomorrow some stupid boy who wasn't worth it. Before you knew it, Zoe would be cracking Bud Light bottles on the mechanical bull and asking for challengers.

Stomping over to them, I said, "Stop hitting each other or no one gets the doll."

They ignored me.

But Dakota/Georgia did drop the cat in the tussle, and Otis was zipping through the kitchen and out the open garage door. Where did he think he was going? At first, as I wrestled to get the doll away from the girls one-handed, I thought he was just trying to escape the sticky, grabby little fingers of five-year-old girls.

Then I got to thinking.

Wasn't it strange that whenever the cat was around, jealousy and selfishness seemed to ooze out of the girls? Not that they were angelic all the time, but it did seem like they were particularly bratty when Otis was on the scene. Maybe he was feeding off their envy.

Maybe he had an agenda.

Or a motive.

Maybe he was trying to use the girls somehow to get the portal open.

That would be seriously not cool.

So I handed my piece of the doll hair over to Levi, who had just come into the room after soccer practice.

"What's going on?" he asked me, looking dumbly at the doll in his hand, his gym bag strapped across his chest.

"Cat fight," I told him. "Gotta go." I fast walked across the kitchen, past Mike, and out the garage door.

I didn't see Otis in the garage and I walked tentatively, afraid of random apple peels inserting themselves under my foot. I really didn't want to break a second arm.

"Kenzie."

I turned, startled, and saw Otis in human form leaning on my mom's minivan. He was smoking a cigarette.

Wonderful. I glanced back at the kitchen, grateful the wall was officially closed again. All I needed was my mother to open the door and see Tattoo Boy inhaling nicotine in what looked like a secret rendezvous with me and I would be grounded until I left for college. Not that I was going to college, but my mother didn't know that.

"You can't be here like that," I told him, thoroughly annoyed. "My mother freaked when I wanted to go out with a nineteen-year-old. If she sees you she's going to have a total cow. What are you, like twenty-four?"

"Twelve hundred, give or take a year."

Yikes. "Which would really make it difficult to explain."

"I'm not interested in you that way. You are definitely too immature for me."

Well, excuse me. "That's not the point! My mother will see you and assume you're here for the wrong reason. You can't exactly pass as a pizza guy since you have no pizza."

"Did Levi tell you about Lilith?"

Of course he hadn't. "That's none of your business."

Otis laughed. "It's cute how you defend him."

We would just ignore that.

"Are you feeding off those little girls' envy?" I asked, disgusted by the thought.

He just shrugged, obviously feeling no shame. "I have to eat."

"Go down the street and hit up some criminal adults for a meal. They're five years old. It's twisted to stir up envy in them."

"I'm a demon, remember? I take what I can get where I can get it."

"Are you really the prison warden? You don't look like a warden."

"I'm sorry." He rolled his eyes. "I should have realized I can only look in human form what your stereotypical idea of a demonic prison warden should be." He put his cigarette out on the floor of the garage, blowing a final stream of smoke in my face, his elbows still on the hood of the minivan.

That's when it hit me. He had appeared to me as a human the first time in the bathtub. A portal. He had never morphed anywhere else, until now. Leaning against the minivan. Another portal.

It wasn't the wall at all, it never had been. It was the van. That's what I had hit the wall with. That's where Otis had first appeared. That's where the apple peel had been, under the front tire. Going through the hole in the wall hadn't allowed the peel to serve as a conduit for the growling guard, the van had.

The van was where I had sprayed my Diet Coke on the radio the day the air portal opened, just like when I had dropped my acne meds in the tub drain and opened the water portal.

I stood up straighter and stared at Otis, my heart pounding. I knew I was right. But I couldn't let him know what I now knew.

"You're right," I said. "That sounds really stupid, doesn't it? By the way, was there something you needed because I have to go back in before someone comes looking for me."

Way to sound helpful and therefore *completely* suspicious.

His eyes did narrow, but he just said, "Meet me here tonight at ten. I can tell you what you need to know to send Levi and me back. I can't reenter the portal without your help, and I'm taking Levi back with me. That's what you want, right?"

I hesitated, but knew what I needed to say. "Yes. That's what I want."

"Because after all, he's been nothing but trouble." Otis's eyes burned in the dim garage, the same amber yellow they had been when he had been fighting with Levi in cat form. "He's gotten you grounded, gotten you stuck doing laundry, babysitting . . . Your friends weren't talking to you and you lost your boyfriend.

All because of Mr. Popular, Levi, who can do no wrong, and who was guilty of the exact same thing you were, cheating on a boyfriend or girlfriend. Yet he walked away without a scratch, didn't he, and you're still paying the price."

I stood still, frozen to the cold concrete in my black and hot pink striped socks, the demon's words wrapping around me like a cold unpleasant mist. Otis was right, about all of those things, and it hurt, it burned, and stirred up anger and jealousy in me. I stared at the van bumper, suddenly feeling small and sad and violated and thinking that maybe, just maybe, Otis was right and I should send Levi back. Hadn't I thought that myself? Hadn't I listed the pros and cons? I had nothing to lose by sending Levi back and everything to gain.

"And why did he do it, do you think? Was it really just spontaneous, kissing you?" Otis asked softly. "Or did he think that maybe with you he could get what Amber wasn't willing to give?"

My head snapped up. What a nasty, dirty, little demon. He'd almost had me going there with his spellbinding words and persuasive, helpful tone of voice. But it was a trick, a manipulation.

"You're right," I said, in a shaky voice, conjuring up a tear and squeezing it out of my right eye. Might as well put the acting skills to use, even if I had the misfortune to only ever be able to fake cry out of my right eye. The left never cooperated. "Meet you here at ten o'clock?"

"Ten o'clock. Remember to bring Levi with you. Tell him you need to talk *privately*." Otis leered at me. "He won't hesitate to take you up on that."

I nodded and gave a sniffle. I stared at the ground and wiped away my fake tear with my injured arm, using the fingertips that were sticking out of the cast. Then I whirled around like I was humiliated and ran into the house, slamming the door for drama.

He he he. Not bad. I took a curtsy for my performance and laughed to myself about the fact that Otis back in cat form would be stuck in the garage until he scratched and someone let him in.

Kenzie Sutcliffe vs. Demonic Creatures, Round 2. Ring the bell.

I was so sending Otis's butt back to hell.

At nine I snuck out to the minivan and put my purse on the front passenger seat and stuck the keys in the ignition. Using a screwdriver and keeping an eye on the kitchen door, I pried the faceplate off the satellite radio and contemplated its guts. I wasn't sure how to disconnect it, so I figured I would just cut the wires when the time came. Ducking back into the kitchen, I grabbed scissors, then left the driver's door to the van open, but pushed it so that it looked closed. I also opened the garage door and prayed the TV was on loud enough that no one in the house would notice, or it wouldn't register to anyone's frazzled post-dinnertime brains what the sound actually meant.

Back in the house, I lay down on my bed, fully clothed, including shoes, and rested my cast on my chest. Eyes closed, listening to my iPod on shuffle, I contemplated all the ways my plan could go seriously wrong.

It took a while, because there were some serious Grand Canyon–size holes in my plan. But that had never stopped me before, and I figured until a demon slayer magically appeared out of the sky and handed me a manual, I was going to have to stumble my way through this on my own. Which pretty much guaranteed a boatload of mistakes were going to be made.

I felt someone's eyes on me, so I opened them and almost screamed to see Levi bent over me about six inches from my face. "What are you doing? Get away from me!"

"I thought you were dead!" he said, holding his chest like he was having a heart attack. "What are you doing?"

"I'm lying here. How could you think I was dead? I'm lip-synching!"

"It's dark in here. You don't have your light on and I couldn't see your lips moving. You weren't moving at all. What am I supposed to think?"

"That I want to be alone. Which I do. Go away." I rolled on my side, hoping he'd get the very obvious hint.

"What happened with Zoe and Georgia . . . that's not cool," he said.

I couldn't really see his expression in the dark, but I could feel his worry. I had never doubted that in his weird way, Levi cared about my sister. "No, it's not. But I have it under control."

The minute the words left my mouth, I realized I shouldn't have said anything at all. There was a big long pause, and then he said, "Kenzie. What are you planning?"

"Nothing. Nothing at all. What would I be planning?" I played with the edge of my comforter.

Another big old pause. "Don't do anything stupid."

"Who, me? Please. I've never done a single stupid thing in my whole life."

Chapter Fourteen

The stupid thing I was planning to do had to take place after the kindergartner and the parents were in bed but before the prearranged meeting with the demon cat. It was tricky timing, but Zoe went to bed at nine, and my parents were in their room with the door shut and locked by nine thirty, which lead me to believe they were occupied in ways I didn't want to consider. However, that did mean they probably wouldn't hear the back door opening and the minivan leaving the garage.

I wasn't worried about my brother, Brandon. He was hermited in his room most of the time—hence the need to use his shirt as a tissue—and paid attention to no one but himself for the most part. When I snuck down the hall at nine forty-five, I paused outside his bedroom door. I didn't hear Brandon at all, and I could hear Levi talking, presumably to Amber on his cell phone, because there were pauses in the conversation and he was saying things like "I don't care what skirt you wear as long as it's short."

It was pretty safe to say he wouldn't be suggesting that to Brandon.

I rolled my eyes at the piggish comment. Ten bucks said Amber was giggling on the other end.

Moving as silently as I could into the family room, I paused to let my eyes adjust to the darkness. A white cat shouldn't be too hard to find in the dark, right? But I stood there for a good five minutes scoping out the room and I didn't see Marshmallow Pants aka Otis at all. I was about to get seriously annoyed when I felt a telltale rub against my ankle.

The stupid demon had strolled right up to me. I didn't even hesitate.

With a speed I didn't even know I was capable of, I bent over, snagged Otis with my good right arm and tucked him against my chest and cast as I dashed across the kitchen. In one minute or less, I had him out of the house, in the garage, and into the waiting minivan.

And straight into the animal crate my mother had bought for him the week before.

He resisted as he realized what was happening, but I had the element of surprise on my side, and I crammed his furry butt in and slammed the door shut. I slid the van door closed, hopped into the open driver's side, and turned the key in the ignition as quietly as I could. Not that you can start a car quietly, but I was hopeful. I shifted gears, eased off the brake, and backed up. It was difficult to switch into reverse while holding on to the wheel since I had a big honking cast in the way, but I figured once I was in drive, I wouldn't need to shift gears anymore since it was an automatic.

Otis meowed and snarled and swatted at his crate door.

I wanted to tell him to shut up, but frankly I was too freaked out and pumped up on adrenaline. Cruising down the street, I tried to go fast enough to get where I was headed before my hair went gray, but not so fast that I would get pulled over.

I was rolling up to the stop sign at the entrance to our neighborhood when I heard Levi's voice.

"What are you *doing*? Are you insane?"

Ack! Why was he in the van? I whipped my head around. "Me? What are you doing here? You were just on the phone with Amber!"

Levi was climbing over the crate from the backseat. He plunked down on the passenger seat, tossing my purse to the floor. My lip gloss rolled out onto the floor mat and he didn't even bother to pick it up. If he lost me a ten-dollar lip gloss I was taking it out of his demon bank account.

"I faked the phone call because I knew you were up to something. Don't you dare pull this car out onto the main road," he said, his finger coming up. "You have a broken arm."

"My right arm works."

"Kenzie Anne. You cannot drive this minivan with that huge cast."

He had no right to trot out the middle name like I was his kid. "Levi, I have something to do. If you want to drive me, fine. But you have two seconds to agree and get into this driver's seat or I'm hitting the gas pedal. Your choice."

"You're insane," he repeated. "Tell me what you're doing."

"No. You're either in or you're not." I eased my foot a little off the brake.

"Fine!" He stuck his hand out. "Put it in park. I'll drive wherever you want—just don't be stupid enough to drive yourself."

I parked the car but waited for him to get out of the passenger seat. He didn't. We both stared at each other. "Get out," I said.

"No, you get out."

"How stupid do you think I am? I'll get out and you'll just drive the car off," I said.

"Same for you, chica. I'm not getting out of this car."

"So we'll have to switch inside the car."

Which meant we wound up crawling all over each other, tangled legs and arms and cast, sweat dampening my hair as we jostled around. Finally we both flopped into our switched seats and Levi glared at me. "This is nuts. Where are you taking this cat?"

"Just drive. I'll tell you where to turn." It took nine of the most agonizing and cat-complaining-filled minutes of my life to get to the field that was my destination. Fortunately, Levi didn't ask me any more questions, though he did say something in Latin to Otis, who hissed at him. I had Levi pull into a parking lot, then jump the asphalt and park on the grass under the giant tower that hosted the local radio station. There had been controversy about leaving the tower after suburban development, but it was still there, still broadcasting, and still sending out radiation or whatever the issue was into our child-thick residential community.

The plan was to tune the radio in the car to the station the tower belonged to. And then rip the radio out of the minivan. With my limited knowledge of science, I was trying to go on pure logic. I had opened a water portal with acne meds down the drain and had closed it by destroying the plumbing that ran to the shower. So the theory was that if opening the air portal had occurred with the collision of Diet Coke and radio waves, destroying the signal the same way should close it.

Sucky plan? Yes. But what else did I have going on?

Nothing, really. Might as well risk further parental punishment by stealing their minivan, driving with a broken arm and without a license, and busting up Dad's satellite radio that had become like his fourth child. Okay, technically Levi was driving, but we hadn't gotten permission to take the car or the cat, and it was ten o'clock on a school night. Oh, yeah, and I was still grounded.

Fast track to trouble. I was so good at it.

"Why are we in a field?"

"Why didn't you tell me the minivan was the portal?" I shot back.

Levi had the decency to look guilty. "I couldn't, you know that! But hey, you're brilliant. I knew you'd figure it out."

Flattery would get him nowhere, but I did suddenly realize what having Levi in the car meant. "This is a radio station. I'm going to close the portal by tossing soda on the radio as we get the signal from right above us. You know what that means, right?"

He shot me a totally undecipherable look.

I turned on the radio and started searching for the right station. If this worked, Levi would get sucked back in right along with Otis. I knew it. He knew it.

I hit buttons harder, my heart pounding. I couldn't find the station in my panic. Levi wasn't saying anything and I knew he was going to let me decide whether to send him back or not.

I just couldn't do it. There was no way. "Get out of the car, Levi. Run behind the bus shelter over there. Now, I'm serious!"

"You want me to stay?" he asked, giving me a searching look.

"Yes, moron, go!" I was having a hard time breathing and the screeching sounds Otis was making were wearing my nerves down to nothing. "Don't make me regret it! Go!" If he didn't get out, I was going to shove him out or just let him get sucked up. Either way it wasn't going to be pretty.

But Levi shot me a grin, leaned over and kissed me full, long, and hard, then jumped out of the car. I could hear his feet pounding as he ran across the pavement. I finally found the station and some weird polka music came blaring out of the speakers. I cranked it even louder, wincing at the enthusiastic accordion riff, and closed my eyes for a second to collect my mental strength. Then I popped open the can of Diet Coke in the cup holder, turned and undid the latch to the cat crate, and opened my passenger door in rapid succession.

The next two minutes happened so fast, if I had had time to

think I probably would have freaked and screamed, but there was no time to even suck in a breath, let alone let a shriek rip. Even before I had the passenger door open, Otis came flying out of the crate at me with his claws out and teeth bared. I raised my cast to block him, and with my right hand I splashed the radio with my Diet Coke and cut the wires. The scissors got knocked to the floor when I found myself with a human Otis on top of me, both of us piled into the passenger seat.

For a split second he was in front of me, crushed against my chest, liquid dripping from his shiny pointed teeth inches from my eyes, his face so close I could count the hairs in his goatee, his eyes burning bright yellow, angry and venomous.

Then I felt a sucking sensation, air swirling all around me, and heard a horrible moaning that reminded me of the first time I had closed the water portal. With shaky fingers, I pressed back against the seat and clicked my seatbelt in place, fighting the urge to push Otis off of me. Better to just leave him alone and see what happened.

That was a mistake.

He grabbed onto my cast and I felt a piercing pain rip through my arm that made me yelp out loud. I looked down, trying to wrestle my arm away from him, and saw a white light shooting off of his fingertips and racing over my cast. I had no idea what he was doing, but it was agonizing, tears instantly pooling in my eyes, panic rising in my gut.

I pushed weakly at him with my right arm, but he wasn't moving.

Suddenly Levi appeared next to me in the open door, standing outside the van, and he punched Otis in the face, hard, loosening the demon's grip on me.

"Levi, let go!" I shrieked, aware even through the pain that the portal was closing. I could hear the grind and twist and turn, feel the air sucking backward in the van.

But Levi hit Otis again, knocking him back against the windshield and forcing him to drop his hold on me. I undid my seatbelt, wiggled out from under him, and catapulted myself back toward the cat crate, stumbling and falling, but getting out of the way. My first instinct was to get out of the van, but somehow I knew I had to be there, inside, for the portal to close.

Levi had paused to see that Otis wasn't reaching for me, and then I saw his face drop down and disappear, like he had crawled under the car. The passenger door slammed shut. Otis looked at me and opened his mouth to speak, his hand reaching out for me. His fingers got within inches of my throat when he was suddenly ripped backward, the wind swirling inside the car. It stung my eyes and I closed them, clinging to the seat behind me for support. It felt like my hair and clothes were going to be torn off by the force of the air sucking past me, and I braced my feet against the back of the driver's seat.

When the wind died down thirty seconds later, and I pried my dry eyes open, there was no Otis in the van with me. The cat crate was on its side and everything from my purse was rolling around on the floor, but there was neither cat nor human Otis. I blinked at the tampon and the gel pen cruising my way between the seats.

The silence after the noise was strange and I just sat there, frozen, breathing hard, processing. The radio had gone dead.

Levi's head popped up in the passenger side window and then he pulled the door open, checking out the inside of the minivan.

"Dude," he said with a big grin. "He's gone. You did it again, K-Slay!"

I had. And the nickname was starting to grow on me. I sat up. "All in a day's work." It would have sounded blasé and tough except I kind of squeaked it out and sounded like I might burst into tears at any second, which I thought I might.

My arm was throbbing and I had a runny nose from the wind.

Levi reached out a hand and helped me up from the floor. When I was settled in the passenger seat, he scooped up everything rolling around and shoved it all back into my purse. "We should probably take you back to the ER," he said. "He twisted your arm hard, didn't he?"

"Yes. It does hurt, but can't it wait until tomorrow? It's already broken. What could he have done to it, right?" At the moment, I just wanted to savor my victory and then go to bed.

"We can do that." Levi clicked my seatbelt in and smiled at me. "You're crazy, you know that?"

How was that news? "I know. But have you looked at my father? I come by it honestly." I rested my head back on the seat and sighed. "Man, I deserve new jeans after this. And I think I need to change my hair dye again."

"Blue tips?" he asked.

"Purple."

"With your coloring?" He raised an eyebrow, but there was a look in his eye that said he was teasing me. "But whatever, it's your hair."

I stuck my tongue out at him. "Purple."

He came around the front of the van and got into the driver's seat, belted himself, and put the car in reverse. "You're beautiful, you know that?"

He said it with such seriousness and so out of nowhere that I couldn't even make myself scoff at him because there was a big lump in my throat, and the tears that I had thought were gone suddenly came back tsunami-style. I swiped at them, annoyed. God, I was such a girl.

No clue what to say, I settled for a strangled, "Thanks."

"And the new jeans are on me because you rocked tonight."

"Demon bank going to let you withdraw enough to cover my taste?" I asked.

"I'll work it out." He glanced over at me, serious. "You could have sent me back. You didn't."

"No."

And neither of us said anything else about it the rest of the way home.

When we pulled into the garage, my father appeared in the doorway in his flannel pajama pants and a navy blue T-shirt. "Where exactly have the two of you been?" he demanded, loud enough that we heard him through the closed doors of the van.

"Uh-oh," I whispered. "Not good." And I was so glad Levi was driving instead of me. That probably would have been like

signing my own death certificate to roll into the garage driving il-
legally wearing a cast.

"No problem." Levi reached out and squeezed the fingertips
of my broken arm. "I've got your back."

My heart did a funny weird flip-flop in my chest. "You sure?"

"Yep." Levi got out of the car and said, "Hey, Mr. S. Didn't
mean to scare you, but the cat ran away. Kenzie and I saw him and
we decided to see if we could snag him by following in the car."

"The cat ran away?" My dad looked kind of excited at the
prospect of losing Marshmallow Pants. "Why didn't you come and
get us?"

"We knocked on your door," Levi said as we went into the
house. "But you didn't answer."

"Oh, ah, we were sleeping."

Ohmigod, was my dad blushing? If I hadn't been so grossed
out, I would have laughed.

"Right," Levi said.

"Did you get the cat back?" Dad asked.

"Nope. I think he's gone for good. You know how cats are.
They just move on and never show up again."

We could only hope.

"That's too bad," Dad said, clearly trying to contain his glee
and not really succeeding.

"Yeah, it's awful," I said. "Good night."

I wanted my dad to go back to bed. For some reason, I wasn't
feeling triumphant about closing the portal. It felt like there was a
loose end. Even when Levi walked me upstairs and said, "You did

awesome," I still didn't feel like I was ready to accept that it was over and just go to bed.

After Levi retreated into Brandon's room, and I had brushed my teeth, I realized what it was. My original plan had called for me to yank the radio out of the car and dispose of it.

Clearly that wasn't necessary, but it had seemed like a good idea. It still did. Totally get rid of all evidence of portal openage.

So with minty-fresh breath, I went back downstairs and crept into the garage. Since I had already cut all the wires, it was just a matter of lifting it out and off its stand. My father was going to require an explanation, which I didn't have, but I would deal with that later. Going out the side door of the garage with the radio in my good hand, I dropped it in the trash can nestled between my mother's dead tomato plants and the walkway to the front of the house.

Then in a moment of inspiration, I ran back in, got matches, tossed some leaves off the ground into the garbage can, and dropped the match in. It went up with a nice satisfying poof, and I watched the crackle and burn of the leaves and smelled the rubbery stench of the radio smoldering.

Now *that* was a moment of triumph. I felt the closure I hadn't in the van and stood there in the dark, cold night feeling a little gleeful. Yeah, I was a demon slayer. So take that, Otis / Botis / Marshmallow Pants, evil cat from hell.

Levi's head came out of the garage. "What are you doing now? I swear, I need to put a bell on you like a dog."

"Very funny. Who is Lilith, by the way?" He had never answered that little question.

"I have no idea," he said, bouncing a soccer ball on his knee. "And what are you doing?"

Right. He didn't know who Lilith was. Please. But I let it go, feeling too satisfied with myself and my night's work. "I'm burning the radio. It feels really good." I bent my head back and sucked in some cold November air. "Ahh. It's a good night for a fire."

Levi dropped the soccer ball he'd been holding. "*What?* You're *burning* the radio?"

Something about his tone made me lose some of my enthusiasm for the project. "Yes. Why?"

He didn't answer, just went back into the garage. A minute later, he reappeared with the fire extinguisher. "Put it out."

"Why?"

"Why do you think?" He looked at my gimp hand. "Here, just press the nozzle with your good hand."

I tried, but my fingers slipped and I sprayed foam all over the front of Levi. "Sorry." I wanted to laugh but bit my lip instead.

"This isn't funny."

"Yes, it is. How stupid do we look out here?"

"About as stupid as two people who just opened a new portal." He looked pointedly at me. "Which you just did."

"What?" Was he saying . . .

I glanced down at the radio. Burning. On the point right outside the family room that I had mapped on my pentagram diagram as one of the five points. "Fire . . . um, Levi, did I just do what I think I did, that I don't want to say out loud?"

"It's highly likely," he said.

Huh. Maybe I wasn't going to be gifted with new jeans after all.

"Oops."

"You know this is going to keep happening, don't you?"

"What?" I knew what he meant, but with a little luck—haha, when did I ever have that?—maybe he just meant my clumsiness was going to continue, not that portals were going to keep opening.

"Portals are going to keep opening."

Blech. "So, basically you're saying I have to keep doing this like over and over again?"

He nodded prosaically. "Yep. Till we figure out how to close all five simultaneously."

I gave the garbage can one more shot with the fire extinguisher. "Wow, what a fun high school career for me. Can I put demon slayer on my application for drama school? I think this applies under the extracurricular activities as a charitable endeavor."

"Not if you want them to think you're sane, but you can probably write an original monologue for auditions. They'll think you're mega-creative."

"Good call." We stared at the fizzled fire and burnt-out radio, both thoughtful. I should have been more worried than I was, but at some point resignation had set in. Call me K-Slay.

"Lilith was my fiancée," Levi said suddenly.

I whipped my head around to stare at him. "Are you serious? You were *engaged*? At sixteen?" Yikes.

"Yep. It was arranged by higher-ups, you know. I wasn't given a choice."

He frowned, and I wasn't feeling a huge sense of loss on his part for whatserface. "Not that choice matters," I said. "Who is capable of picking a spouse that you're stuck with for eternity at sixteen?"

Or any age. Look at divorce rates.

"If I'd have been given a choice, I wouldn't have picked her. You know I actually voluntarily put myself in prison to avoid tying the knot with that clinging nag?"

I stared at him. "You took incarceration over marriage?" Now *that* was funny. I burst out laughing.

He grinned back at me, clearly not offended. "I had to do what I had to do. Trust me, you'd have done the same thing. But now I'm here, and I have a choice to be with whoever I want."

My laughter died out. There seemed to be an implied insult there. "So you're choosing to date Amber."

It wasn't a question. He was dating Amber.

But he leaned closer to me, with those smoldering green eyes, and my heart started to race again, in a good way.

"Not Amber. That's over. I want to choose *you*, but I'm not sure how you feel about that."

How did I feel about that? Sort of like helium had inflated my lungs and I might lift off the ground at any given moment. Not logical, but there it was, and I was going to roll with it.

"I guess since I kept you here, I might as well make use of you."

Levi laughed, and then he kissed me, the kind where you forget your name, your phone number, and even the English language. He pressed me against the house, which was good, since my legs no longer seemed capable of supporting my weight.

"Can this really work between a demon and a demon slayer?" I asked, proud of myself for admitting my slayer status.

"It just might be a beautiful disaster," he said, his lips near my ear.

Creating disasters was something I was fabulous at, so why not, right?

Printed in the United States
by Baker & Taylor Publisher Services

Printed in the United States
by Baker & Taylor Publisher Services